Wings to Fly

Wings to Fly

Celia Barker Lottridge

•

ILLUSTRATIONS BY
Mary Jane Gerber

A Groundwood Book
DOUGLAS & McINTYRE
VANCOUVER TORONTO BUFFALO

Groundwood Books / Douglas & McIntyre Ltd.
585 Bloor Street West, Toronto, Ontario M6G 1K5

Distributed in the U.S.A. by Publishers Group West
4065 Hollis Street, Emeryville, CA 94608

Library of Congress data is available

Canadian Cataloguing in Publication Data

Lottridge, Celia B. (Celia Barker)
Wings to fly

"A Groundwood book".
ISBN 0-88899-293-9 (bound) ISBN 0-88899-280-7 (pbk.)

I. Title.
PS8573.0855W56 1997 jC813'.54 C97-930533-0
PZ7.L67Wi 1997

Illustrations by Mary Jane Gerber
Design by Michael Solomon
Printed and bound in Canada by Webcom

The publisher gratefully acknowledges the assistance of the Canada Council
and the Ontario Arts Council

THE CANADA COUNCIL | LE CONSEIL DES ARTS
FOR THE ARTS | DU CANADA
SINCE 1957 | DEPUIS 1957

For my aunts,
Lucile Barker Kane and Amandalee Barker Knoles,
with thanks for their stories about their young years
near Provost, Alberta.

ONE

"Whoa, Ginger," said Josie.
The sturdy bay pony halted in the dusty wagon track. She was used to resting for a moment in this spot because Josie always stopped here to look across the fields at the silver house. Even today when her brother Sam was far ahead of her in a tearing hurry to get to town, she could take just a minute to admire it.

The silver house stood all alone on a small rise of ground. It didn't have even a chicken house to keep it company or a path to invite a traveler to its door. Nothing around it moved except the prairie grass stirring gently in the hot wind. Today it seemed to Josie that the house was just lightly settled on the earth like a big gray bird. At any moment it might spread its wings and slowly fly away, back to a place where such houses were common.

Of course the house was not really silver. It was built of unpainted boards that had weathered to a soft, silvery gray. The house Josie lived in was built of weathered wood, too, but nails had been pounded into it, snowballs thrown against it, and clotheslines attached to it. It looked like a house that had been well used for three years by five people, and by horses who loved to rub against it to get the flies off.

But no one had ever lived in the silver house. Josie knew the story. Mr. Ranald McLeod had come to the Curlew district from Ontario just like thousands of other homesteaders. He had worked for three years to prove up his claim and build a house for his bride who would come from back east as soon as it was finished. Josie thought that he must have loved her very much, because he had built a fine house. It wasn't big—no homesteader could afford the lumber for a big house— but it was not a one-story box like the other houses around Curlew. It had an upstairs with two dormer windows, one in front and one in back, as well as curly gingerbread trim under the eaves, and a wide front porch.

On a hot day like this, Josie liked to imagine sitting on that porch with a glass of cool lemonade in her hand, looking out over the wide prairie landscape. There would be no chores to do, no one to hustle her out to pump water or bring in the washing.

Josie heard hoofbeats and looked down the track. It was Sam, of course. He was taking the chance to get King up to a gallop for a few minutes. In this weather Pa always said, "Let the horses take it easy when they can." But Sam couldn't resist an excuse to go fast.

"The train will be here in five minutes," he said. "We shouldn't be wasting time."

"I know," said Josie. She pressed her bare heels into Ginger's round sides and the pony reluctantly started trotting at a gentle pace. Sam turned King and rode alongside.

The track had been worn through the prairie grass by horses and wagons. In the three years the Ferriers had lived near the town of Curlew it had gotten wide enough for two horses side by side. Josie could remember when it was so faint and narrow that it could barely be seen in some places. Now Pa said that soon it would be a proper road and then, maybe, they could get a Model T Ford.

Sam looked over at Josie. "Why do you like to look at that house so much?" he asked idly.

Josie thought for a minute. "It's special," she said. "It's like a house from far away that got here accidentally. And it's so sad that Mr. McLeod doesn't live in it. Somebody should. It's the best house around here."

She didn't tell Sam that she always thought of Mr. McLeod's lost bride. She was the sad part of the story of the house. Not that she had died. No, she had come from Ontario when the house was ready, down to the fancy brass doorknobs. She arrived at Curlew station with her trunks. Mr. McLeod met her, of course, and drove her straight out to the house.

People said that she sat in the wagon for a long time and looked at the little wooden house and the land around it, flat and treeless as far as the eye could see. Then she said, "I can't live here. Take me back to the station." She took the next train east to Ontario, and Mr. McLeod never went into the house again. He still lived in a boarding house in town and came along this very track to farm his land, but he left the house alone.

Josie wondered whether his bride ever thought of him now. Did she ever wish she had given the house a chance?

"You're quiet," Sam said curiously. "Are you thinking about ghosts?"

"Ghosts?" said Josie. "Are you trying to scare me? Why would the silver house have ghosts?"

Sam looked a little embarrassed. "I guess it's just because it's empty. It always seems a little spooky to me, as if it's waiting for something. It makes me think of that old house we used to ride past back in Iowa. Everybody said it was haunted."

Josie frowned. She barely remembered a little falling-down house that stood alone in a field near their old farm, but she had been just eight years old when the Ferriers left Iowa. Sam had been nearly twelve.

"Haunted?" she said. "Nobody told me."

"Mama wouldn't let us scare you with ghost stories," said Sam. "Anyway, this house is different. It just reminds me because it's empty." He looked down the track. "We're almost in town. I can see the water tower. See you at Pratt's." He nudged King into a gallop again and rode on ahead.

Josie squinted her eyes against the dust they stirred up. She didn't have to hurry Ginger. Sam wanted to get to the station in time to see the train pull in. He would help Mr. Pratt, the postmaster, unload the bags of mail and lug them over to Pratt's Dry Goods, Grocery and Post Office. In return Mr. Pratt would pick out the Ferriers' mail right away.

In the meantime Josie had plenty of time to get the canning jars and spices Mama needed to make pickles. For the first time since coming to Canada she had managed to raise a proper garden and now she had plenty of cucumbers but no jars.

Once they had passed the houses at the edge of

town Josie slowed Ginger to an ambling walk. Curlew was just three blocks of stores and businesses and a few short streets of houses but there might be something interesting to see. She passed the hotel and the restaurant and the laundry. The bakery was always tempting, but Mama did her own baking. The newspaper office came next. Mr. Murray, the editor of the Curlew *Star*, was a friend of Josie's. She had won a contest for the best essay on "The Future of Alberta," and it had been printed in the paper. On the glorious day it was published, Mr. Murray had invited Josie to the office and given her the first copy of the newspaper as it came off the press. Josie loved the organized clutter of the newspaper office, and she sometimes dropped in to chat. Today there wasn't really time.

She rode on past the livery stable where horses could be boarded, hired, bought or sold. Beside it was the blacksmith shop. Josie could see a glow of fire through the open doors, where a group of men and boys gathered around a horse being shod. It must be hot in there on such a day.

Josie arrived at Pratt's store without seeing anything more interesting than a dog rolling in the dust. She guessed that everyone was down at the station waiting for the train from Winnipeg. There were still settlers coming in, though Pa said that the best land was gone. At least now, in 1918, they would find a bit more of a town than Josie had seen the first time she had set eyes on Curlew. Then there had been almost nothing between the station and Pratt's.

Josie slid off Ginger's back and led her over to the watering trough on the shady side of the store building. Ginger drank for a long time, then shook her head and snorted loudly.

"You're welcome," said Josie. She led the pony to the front of the store and tied her reins to the railing.

The inside of the store seemed dark after the glare of the morning sun. Josie blinked and saw Mrs. Pratt standing behind the dry goods counter measuring out some bright-yellow gingham for a small, tidy woman.

She smiled at Josie. "I suppose you've come for the mail?" she said.

"Yes," said Josie. "Sam's down at the station helping Mr. Pratt. But Mama needs some things, too, especially pickling jars."

"I'll be with you in a minute," said Mrs. Pratt.

"I don't have to hurry," said Josie. "I'll just look around." She began to walk the length of the store, first up the food side where barrels of crackers and flour stood beneath shelves of canned goods and packets of baking soda and Bird's Custard Powder. When she passed the pickle barrel the sharp smell made her mouth water. The oatmeal cookies heaped in a wooden box on the counter smelled delicious, too, but she had no money to spend on extras.

The back of the store was filled with men's work boots and overalls, but next to them was a short rack of ready-made dresses and shelves of many-colored bolts of cloth. There were spools of ribbon and rickrack and shallow drawers filled with thread, pins and other notions, all neatly labeled. Josie had no knack for sewing, as Mama put it, but she loved to imagine all the beautiful things that could be made.

Farther along were the cases full of the most interesting things of all—toys and knives and pencil cases—things children might buy, if they had money in their pockets.

Mrs. Pratt was handing the customer her parcel. "I know your little girl will look ever so pretty in her new dress," she said. Then she turned to Josie. "You say your mother is making pickles?" she said. "Will you be needing vinegar and salt as well as jars?"

"Just the jars," said Josie. "And these spices, if you have them." She handed Mrs. Pratt a list Mama had made.

Mrs. Pratt pushed her glasses down on her nose and read, "Turmeric or allspice. We have allspice but not turmeric. Mustard seed and celery seed we have, of course, but no stick cinnamon. It hasn't come in. I'll send cloves instead. I think they will do very well."

Josie hoped so. Mama wanted to make her special bread and butter pickles. For the past two years either the bugs or the crows had got to the cucumbers before they were big enough for pickles, but now there was a basket of them waiting at home to be doused with vinegar and spices. Josie's mouth watered again.

Just as Mrs. Pratt was getting a box of quart canning jars out of the back room, Sam came in with Mr. Pratt. They were lugging heavy canvas mail bags. Mr. Pratt puffed as he heaved a bag over the post office counter. "The Eaton's summer sale catalogues are in," he said. "That makes for heavy mail. I'm sure glad young Sam came along to help."

Eaton's catalogue! Josie forgot about being hungry. It was a great day when a catalogue came. The whole family would go through it over and over again, picking out what they wanted, then changing their minds. Most things they never did get, but it was fun to think about.

What Josie especially liked was playing with the catalogues after the wishing and ordering were done. Luckily Matt, who was about to turn nine, still liked to join her in cutting out the pictures of well-dressed men, women and children and sorting them into families or whole towns full of citizens of all ages. Sometimes they cut the heads off and switched them around to make more interesting people or drew beards on the men and smudges on the faces of the children to make them look less refined. Matt's favorite game was to choose a crew to go on a voyage of exploration and then, in the back of the catalogue, find all the supplies they would need. Josie always made sure he included at least one girl, as a regular crew member, not as cook.

Sam brought in the last mail bag. He looked over at Josie and said, "There's a new family come in on the train. They're from England and they seem sort of lost. The girl is about your age. Could you go and talk to her?"

"From England?" The very thought made Josie feel a little shy but also curious. "Don't they know anyone here?"

"No," said Sam. "It's just like it was for us when we came from Iowa. I asked them if they knew the Martingales. I guess it was stupid to think of it just because the Martingales come from England, too. Anyway, they don't know them or anyone else. They're over at the livery stable buying a wagon and a horse."

Josie went out into the bright sunshine and looked across the street. She could see Chalkey Pratt who owned the livery stable, talking to a tall man wearing a dark jacket and cap. A woman and a girl stood near-by beside a heap of trunks and boxes.

Josie crossed the dusty street. The woman didn't seem to notice her at all. She was staring into the distance as if she didn't want to look at anything nearby. The girl watched Josie anxiously. She had dark eyes and very pale skin. Her brown hair was smoothed back from her face and braided into one long thick braid that hung over her shoulder. Was she hoping that Josie would speak to her or that she wouldn't? Josie couldn't tell, but she smiled anyway and the girl smiled back uncertainly.

Josie almost said, "Welcome to Curlew," but that seemed like something the mayor would say, so instead she said, "Hello. I think my brother Sam spoke to you at the station. He says that you've just come from England. I'm very glad to meet you. My name is Josie Ferrier."

The woman didn't seem to hear her. The girl looked at her mother and then at Josie. Her face turned a little pink and she stopped smiling but she said, "I'm Margaret Graham. This is my mother, and my father is over there. We need a horse and wagon, it seems."

"Oh, yes," said Josie, "you must have a horse. A

team of horses really. We came from Iowa so we brought two horses with us, but we had to get another team for working and then another horse because there was no other way to get to school. Now we have six. That's Ginger over there. She's not a horse really. She's a pony but she's only half a hand smaller than a horse." She suddenly realized that she was chattering about herself. "It's very interesting that you're from England," she said. "We have some neighbors from England but they don't sound quite like you."

Mrs. Graham suddenly spoke. "There are a great many different accents in England, child," she said. "We come from Sussex, in the south. They probably come from some other part."

"From near Manchester, I think," said Josie. "I looked it up on a map once. It didn't look so far from London."

"Manchester is quite, quite different from London," said Mrs. Graham firmly. "Or from Sussex."

Josie was confused. Had she been rude? Mrs. Graham sounded quite angry. She looked back at Margaret and immediately forgot about Mrs. Graham. Margaret looked unhappy enough to cry.

Josie gathered her wits. "I don't know very much about England," she said. "But I could tell you about Curlew. Where are you going to settle?"

"My father has bought some land. I think it is about four miles from town and it has a house on it. A special sort of house. It's called a soddy." As she talked, Margaret's face looked brighter, but Josie's heart sank. She knew already that Mrs. Graham would hate a house built of blocks of earth.

Just then Mr. Graham came over. He was a tall man with a quiet face. He smiled at Josie.

Margaret said, "Father, this is Josie. She could tell us a bit about Curlew."

"How do you do, Josie," said Mr. Graham. "As you can see, we're completely new to your part of the world. How long have you lived here?"

"Three years," said Josie. "We came from the States. My father bought land from the railroad and we built a house and a barn. Our place is about five miles from town."

"We bought land from a man called Wilks," said Mr. Graham. "Did you know him? I understand he's moved farther west."

"No," said Josie. "But I'm sure Pa did and I do know where his place is. It's out in our direction but a little nearer town than we are. You'll take the right-hand fork in the track where we go left."

Mrs. Graham spoke sharply. "Have you seen this land?" she asked. "Do you know the house?"

Josie was very glad that she had never seen Mr. Wilks' house so that she could honestly say, "No, I've never been by that way. But it would be an easy ride from our place. I'll come and visit you." She turned to Margaret. "I could come by on the first day of school. We could go together."

"Oh, yes," said Margaret. "I'd like that very much. Does school start soon, then?"

"It's a little strange here because of the winter," said Josie. "We can't have school in January and February, so we have it in July and August." She saw that the Grahams all looked puzzled so she explained. "It's so cold in the middle of winter that it's really not safe for the little children to be out on the prairie, going to and from school, you know. Anyway, the first day of the summer session is the Monday after next. I hope you'll be in my class. I've been the only girl ever since the school opened. How old are you?"

"I'm eleven but I'll be twelve soon," said Margaret.

"Perfect," said Josie. "You're just my age so I'm sure you'll be in my class. I'm glad."

She looked across the street and saw Sam coming out of Pratt's laden with bundles. "I have to go now. But if you need anything, come to our place. Just ask anyone where the Ferriers live. They'll tell you."

As she turned to cross the street Josie remembered how small and ugly Curlew had looked to her when she got off the train three years ago. She looked back at Margaret. "Don't worry," she said. "I know that Curlew doesn't look like much but it feels quite friendly when you get to know it. You'll see." Then she said goodbye and went to help Sam tie bundles to King's saddle. As usual, she was riding Ginger bareback, so King had to take the whole load, but he was used to that.

As she rode away she turned to wave at the Grahams, but they had disappeared into the livery stable.

TWO

"Have you ever seen the soddy on Mr. Wilks' place?" Josie asked Sam as they rode toward home.

"I guess I have," said Sam, "but I didn't really notice it. It's just an ordinary soddy. Why?"

"That's where the Grahams are going to live. You know, the new family from England. I don't think they know that a soddy is built of blocks of earth."

"Just like us when we came here. Remember the first time we saw the Chomyks' house? It looked so strange, as if it had just grown up out of the ground. After I visited Gregor a few times I got to kind of like it. It was really warm in winter. But dark because the windows were so small."

"And sod houses are hard to keep clean. I think that's why Mrs. Chomyk wanted Gregor and Mr. Chomyk to build her a wooden house last summer. Sam, Mrs. Graham was wearing white gloves. She's going to hate sweeping a dirt floor."

They were just passing the silver house. Josie looked up at its curtainless windows and thought again of Mr. McLeod's bride. What if Mrs. Graham took one look at the sod house and said, "I'm not living in that. I'm going home."

But of course she couldn't go back to England. It

would cost far too much. People who came to the Curlew district from so far away usually had no money to spare for years afterwards. The journey had used it all.

Josie felt a little mean about it but she was relieved. She was looking forward to having Margaret in her class at school.

By the time they got home Mama had the cucumbers all sliced and was working on the onions.

"Oh, good, you're back," she said. "Did we get any interesting mail?'"

"No letters today," said Josie. "But there's an Eaton's catalogue and Mr. Pratt saved us last week's Edmonton *Bulletins*." She put them aside a little reluctantly and set the canning jars and spices on the table.

"Thank you, Josie," said Mama. "Now you can have this job and I'll take the spices and make up the syrup. Mind you slice the onions as thin as you can."

Josie put on her apron and stood at the round kitchen table working away. She had to be careful because the knife was sharp and onion tears kept filling her eyes. After each half onion was reduced to shreds, she added them to the big bowl where the cucumbers were waiting.

"Who did you and Sam see in town?" Mama asked.

"There's a new family that has bought Mr. Wilks' place. They're from England and they have a girl just my age. Her name is Margaret. Margaret Graham."

"And she'll be the friend you've been wanting? I hope so. It's been hard for you, living so far from town with no girls your age nearby. Sam's been luckier having Gregor down the road."

Josie nodded. Gregor Chomyk was a year older than Sam. He did have two sisters but they were too young to be friends for her. All the other neighbors had been bachelors, until now.

"The Grahams are going to live in a soddy like the Chomyks did, but they don't know anything about sod houses. The Chomyks even knew how to build one. But Mrs. Graham—Mama, she was so dressed up and she wore white gloves. She didn't look happy at all."

Mama looked up from the kettle she was stirring. "This country can be a shock, especially to people from more settled places. It was a little easier for us, I guess. We were used to open fields and being a distance from town. But even for us. . ." She moved the kettle to the side of the stove and sat down opposite Josie. "I'll tell you now, Josie, when I first saw Curlew my heart sank. And when I saw our house, well, I wondered how I could manage to be content in a house that was so little and alone. But Sam and James had worked so hard already. I knew I had to try. I'm sure Mrs. Graham will try, too."

Josie stood holding the knife motionless. "You mean you didn't really like it here at first?" She was amazed. Mama was always—well, almost always— cheerful. It had never occurred to Josie that Mama might sometimes not like what she had to do.

"I wondered whether I would like it. I wasn't at all sure. The house was not just little, it was completely bare. There was so much work to do to make it homelike. Do you remember, Josie? We had to use the parlor drapes to make you a little room to sleep in."

Josie nodded. She remembered that very well. It had made her so cross to find that she had to sleep in the kitchen.

"We're still pretty crowded," said Mama, "but at least you have a room of your own now. So we have made progress."

"I remember that I just sat in your rocking chair and missed my old room and was miserable," said Josie. "Did you miss something a lot?"

"My mother and my sisters," said Mama. "I still miss them. But back then I was used to seeing them every few days. I had never been so alone."

"But you weren't alone. We were here with you, all of us."

"You're right." Mama reached over and squeezed Josie's wrist. "I wasn't alone. But there was no other woman for miles. I could go for weeks without seeing anyone but my family and maybe a neighbor out looking for his cattle. I suppose that sometimes I felt the way you do. I needed a friend who was like me. But there wasn't anyone and I just had to set my mind to doing the best I could. It turned out to be an adventure. It still is."

"Do you think Mrs. Graham can do the same thing?"

"I don't know her, of course, but most women do manage. I'll go to visit her after they get settled. Later she could join the Farm Women's Association or the church ladies group. She doesn't have to face everything alone. And her daughter will have a friend."

She stood up. "I think you've done enough onions. Now we have to salt them down with the cucumbers and let them stand till afternoon. Then we'll cook them up."

Josie went to the wash basin and tried to scrub the onion smell off her hands. Some of it would have to wear off, she decided and shook her hands instead of drying them on the towel. No use making it oniony, too.

She went back to the table and looked longingly at the Eaton's catalogue but it was almost time to set the table for noon dinner. The catalogue deserved at least an hour, so she unfolded an issue of the Edmonton *Bulletin* instead. She started to turn to the page that had stories for children—usually one about a rabbit named Uncle Wiggly. Sometimes now she felt a little old for these stories but she could never resist reading them. But today she glanced at the front page first. There was news about the war in Europe, and several articles about exhibits and entertainment at the Edmonton Exhibition last week. Josie sighed. There wasn't much use reading about it. She had more chance of going to visit Grandma in Iowa than of ever going to Edmonton. But just before she turned the page, a headline caught her eye.

Girl Aviator Flies with Mail from Calgary to Edmonton—Gets Great Reception from Fair Crowd. Josie was intrigued. She knew about aviators, of course. They flew airplanes and put on shows, doing daring loop-the-loops high above the ground. Josie had never seen an airplane herself, but Miss Barnett, the teacher of Curlew School, had seen one at a fair up in Scanda. "They look like giant mosquitoes," she told the children. "It's hard to believe they can lift a human body off the ground. And the aviators do the most amazing things. They even fly upside down. Who knows, maybe some of you boys will grow up to be aviators."

And here was a girl who flew airplanes. Josie sat down to read the article.

"Here she comes," shouted a thousand voices, and twice as many eyes stared into the gray-blue depths of the southern skies."

Josie tried to imagine being in such an enormous crowd of people, all looking in the same direction. Had they really all shouted the same thing? She read on.

"Far away, looking like some great bird, was a speck in the heavens. As it drew nearer it assumed the familiar shape of an airplane ....

"Twice around in a wide circle the machine swung... Then, when it was due west, with the sun behind and the landing place indicated by a huge arrow of white cloth laid out on the grass, the plane tipped its nose downward and swooped like a giant swallow to earth.

"Miss Stinson, disguised in helmet and goggles and wearing an oilskin coat, was plentifully identified by her radiant and irrepressible smile as she stood up in the cockpit of the machine..."

There was more about the crowd cheering and Miss Stinson shaking hands with officials. It wasn't very interesting. Josie wanted to know more about Miss Stinson herself and about her flight. She read on as fast as she could.

"A cross wind from the southwest prevailed all the way making aerial navigation difficult. Miss Stinson traveled at an average height of 6,000 feet .... At six o'clock she passed over Airdrie and the next report was from Red Deer when she was traveling at the rate of 120 miles per hour."

Josie frowned. She knew that trains could go 60 miles per hour. It was impossible to imagine being up in the air going twice that fast. What kind of girl could do such things? And how old was she, anyway?

Josie could tell from the smell of potatoes frying that it was time to set the table but she took a quick look at the front page of the next day's paper. Sure enough, there was a picture of Miss Stinson wearing a stylish hat with the brim turned up on one side. Josie studied it for several minutes. To her the aviator looked like a young woman, not a girl, but she did have a wonderful smile.

At noon dinner she told the family about Katherine Stinson. "I wish I could have seen her. I suppose that after the exhibition she got in her plane and flew away. Imagine that she could do that. Just fly anywhere she wants to go. I'll probably never even get to Edmonton and it's only eighty miles away."

"Maybe she'll come to the fair at Scanda next year," said Matt. "We could go to Scanda. It's only a three-hour drive."

"Possibly we could go," said Pa, "and if we don't, you're sure to have a chance to see an airplane soon. They're the coming thing."

Josie could see that Pa was ready to talk about airplanes but she really didn't care about them very much. It was Katherine Stinson she wanted to see. If only she could meet her. The newspaper hadn't answered any of the important questions. How did she learn to fly? Why did she want to fly in the first place? Was it more exciting or more scary to fly? And how much older than Josie was this girl aviator? Josie ate her corned beef and potatoes much more slowly and quietly than usual.

After the table was cleared and Sam and Matt set to doing their daily turn at dishwashing, she went outside and sat down on the wide steps that Pa had built so that even without a proper porch, they had a place to sit and watch the sunset. Now the sun was high and the sky was higher and clear blue. Josie stared at the sky and thought about Katherine Stinson. She could imagine that an airplane looking like a giant mosquito or maybe a bird might appear out of the west. The pilot would have long hair bundled under a leather helmet and she would look down and see Josie sitting all alone on the steps of a small house plunked in the middle of the vast prairie. She would fly low, circle over the fields and wave. Josie would wave back. And then, before Sam or Mama or anyone had time to come out of the house, the airplane and its pilot would be gone.

THREE

Usually Josie liked getting the *Bulletin* in clumps, but now she wished it would come every day so that she could look for news of Katherine Stinson. But Mr. Pratt had to read it first and then some member of the Ferrier family had to travel into town and bring home all the issues that were waiting for them.

Consequently it was not until July 21 that Josie read "Miss Stinson Flies," a headline that had been printed just after the exhibition ended on July 14. The article described how the aviator had entertained the crowd by taking her airplane up to a height of one thousand feet and circling in "long graceful spirals" and performing "various evolutions above the field." She had shown herself to be "mistress of the machine at all times" and had won the heart of everyone in the crowd.

What Josie liked best was that before the flight "Miss Stinson herself made sure that everything was in running order." Josie tried to imagine her leaning over the engine of the airplane, talking seriously with the mechanics, and fiddling with something the way automobile drivers sometimes did. She still wished the *Bulletin* would tell her how Katherine Stinson had become an aviator, but once the exhibition was over, she simply disappeared from the pages of the newspaper. Josie looked carefully through every issue, just in case.

"Why didn't they tell us more about Katherine Stinson?" she complained one morning at breakfast. "She did something very important."

"Maybe she just flew away and they couldn't ask her any more questions," said Sam. Josie scowled at him.

"News is like that," said Pa. "People want new news every day. They want to read about the war and the prospects for the harvest. Miss Stinson is yesterday's news."

"Not to me," said Josie. "I even asked Mr. Pratt if I could read about her somewhere else. He said she was a bold young woman and should go home where she belongs. She should go by train, he said, and give up silly notions like flying. Why? Why shouldn't she fly a plane?"

"Maybe he thinks it's not the sort of thing a woman should do," said Sam. "Women don't become ship captains or railroad engineers, after all."

"Which may be exactly why she has chosen to be a pilot," said Mama. "No one has thought to tell her she can't do that."

Josie looked at Mama, puzzled. "Who could tell her she can't? What if she just wants to do it and goes ahead?"

Mama sighed. "Well, some things take money," she said. "Buying airplanes, for instance. And often people need to be hired to do what they want to do. You can't be a railroad engineer if no one will give you a job. But there's no doubt that knowing what you want to do and being determined makes a big difference."

"Are you determined to do something, Josie?" asked Matt. "When you grow up, I mean. You're not going to be a pilot, are you?"

"I don't know," said Josie. "I never thought of being a pilot or anything else. Now it turns out I have to be determined." She fell silent. It all sounded very difficult.

"You have time to think about it," said Pa. "No one's going to fly by today and offer you an astonishing new career."

Josie knew it was a joke, but it didn't make her laugh. How could she know what she wanted to do? Until she read about Katherine Stinson she had never thought of wanting to do anything in particular. Did Miss Stinson know she wanted to fly airplanes when she was eleven going on twelve? Josie looked across the table at Sam. He was already thinking about going to university, but what did he want to do later, when he was grown up? She decided to ask him when she got a chance.

Just then Mama looked at the clock on the wall. "Oh, my goodness," she said. "I almost forgot. Miss Barnett is bringing her sister over for a visit this afternoon. I must do the baking before the house gets hot. Josie, after you've cleaned the lamp chimneys, take all the rugs outside and give them a good shake. Sam, when you've pumped water for the horses, bring a bucket in here and wash the floor."

"I'll gather the eggs," said Matt quickly. "May I be excused?" And he was gone before he got an answer.

Mama shook her head. Matt had been known to take most of the morning gathering eggs when house-cleaning was going on.

"Never mind," she said. "He'll be in when the cookies come out of the oven. Then he can polish the silver spoons."

Josie carefully washed the sooty insides of the glass lamp chimneys as she did every day. It was always her job because she had the smallest hands. When they were shining she gathered up the rag rugs. Out in the yard she shook each one so hard that she made a small dust storm all around her. Then she got the big carpet that Mama's rocking chair sat on, hung it over the fence and beat it with a broom.

Did Katherine Stinson have to beat rugs? Surely not. Josie looked up and saw a hawk floating above her, hardly moving its wings.

"How do I look to that hawk?" she wondered. "Just the way I would look to Katherine Stinson if she flew over me in her airplane. Like nothing at all, I guess, or a little dot waving a stick." She waved the broom over her head. "Hello, hawk," she called. "You might meet Katherine Stinson up there some day."

The hawk dipped its wings and soared away in circles, just like Miss Stinson, higher and higher. How would it feel? Josie felt dizzy thinking about it. She hung all the rugs over the fence to wait until the floor was dry.

Noon dinner was slim pickings, as Pa put it. Bread and butter and sliced cucumbers and cold meat left over from Sunday dinner.

"Never mind," said Mama. "There will be pie for

supper and you are all invited to have tea with Miss Barnett and her sister this afternoon. I can do only so much cooking in one day."

"Fair enough," said Pa. "Are you children looking forward to seeing your teacher?"

"Oh, yes," said Josie. Sam and Matt nodded. Miss Barnett was the only teacher Curlew School had had since it opened three years ago. She had taught Matt to read and Josie to do long division and now she was helping Sam get ready for university. She could also build a coal fire to keep the school warm, referee a hockey game, catch ornery horses and even help the children stay calm and cheerful when an early snow-storm threatened to keep them at school overnight. She did that by telling them an exciting story about the ocean.

"You think this is a strong wind," she said. "Well, I remember a storm off the coast of Nova Scotia that blew a great ship right up onto our beach." Then she went on to tell a tale that kept all the children fasci-nated until their fathers came to take them home through the prairie storm.

"I'm looking forward to meeting her sister, too," Josie went on. "I didn't know she had a sister." She was a little surprised to think that she really knew nothing at all about her teacher except that she had come to Alberta from Nova Scotia. "I wonder whether she has more brothers and sisters," she said to Sam. "Do you know?"

"If anybody knew it would be you," said Sam.

It was true. Josie was the one who liked to know about people and she always wanted to know their whole story. But somehow she had never thought of Miss Barnett having a story outside of Curlew School.

At three o'clock the Ferriers were ready for company. They were not wearing their Sunday best but their clothes were fresh and neat and the house was clean and unusually tidy. Mama's china tea set with the blue flowers on it was set out on the round table. The spoons were polished and two cakes and a plate of cookies were waiting. There was also lemonade cooling in a jug hung down the well, for it was a hot end-of-July day.

Mama sat down in the rocking chair and said, "It's a real treat just to sit a while." Josie knew how she felt. They had all rushed through their chores so that they could sit peacefully and visit.

Matt was waiting by the window. "Here they come," he said and ran to open the gate for the buggy. Sam was there to unhitch the horse and lead it to the watering trough. Mama and Josie waited by the door to greet their guests.

"Hello, Mrs. Ferrier. And Josie. It is so good of you to have us for tea. This is my sister, Angela." Miss Barnett gave the young woman beside her a little push, just as she often gave a reluctant student a little push toward the front of the school room for recitation.

Josie looked at Angela Barnett. She was quite different from her sister, she decided. Miss Barnett wore her smooth brown hair in a bun and was brisk and smiling. Angela Barnett had curly red hair and just a few freckles. Her eyes were dark and worried.

"She's pretty," Josie thought. "But why does she look so scared?"

"Come in and sit down," said Mama. "James will be here later. He had to go into town."

"Yes, we passed him on the road," said Miss Barnett. "Angela, these are three of my excellent pupils—Sam, Josie and Matthew."

All together the three young Ferriers said, "How do you do, Miss Barnett." Then they looked at each other with a slight feeling of confusion. It seemed strange to call this young woman Miss Barnett.

Angela Barnett smiled suddenly and stopped looking scared. "Please call me Angela," she said. "I'll have to be called Miss Barnett soon enough. I'm just about to become a teacher, you see. At least for a few weeks."

"Angela is going to teach the summer term at Bruckner School," Miss Barnett explained. "She has just graduated from high school, and she's earning some money to help pay for her university course."

"Where will you go to university, Angela?" asked Mama. "Will you go back to Nova Scotia?"

"I'm going to the University of Alberta," said Angela. "I'm hoping that here in the west women students may have a better chance of being accepted and taken seriously."

"What are you going to study?" said Sam. "Will you go on being a teacher?"

"No," said Angela Barnett in a most definite voice. "I want to be an astronomer."

"You mean study the stars?" said Sam.

"Yes, and the solar system. I've always wanted to

know more about what I see in the sky and I've learned all I can on my own. Now I want to study astronomy seriously."

"Is there a course in astronomy at the university here?" asked Mama.

"Well, first I need basic science and mathematics. Then I might have to go to a larger university and do post-graduate work. It will take a long time and I'll have to keep finding ways to earn money, too. Right now the only way is to teach." She suddenly looked scared again.

"I guess you're worried about teaching." Josie blurted it out and blushed. She was saying the first thing that came into her mind. One of her unfortunate habits, Pa said.

But Angela didn't look offended. She smiled. "I guess it shows," she said. "I just finished being a high school student. It's hard to imagine being the teacher already. But next week I will be."

"I know just how you feel," said Mama. "I had my first school when I was eighteen."

"That's exactly how old I am," said Angela, "and I expect that some of my students will be almost as old."

"They will be," said Mama. "But I can tell you that once you're a teacher the students just naturally think you're an old lady." Miss Barnett smiled in agreement. Mama went on. "Of course, I didn't know that when I was eighteen, and I bought a very sober black hat to make me look older. It was so ugly. I wouldn't wear it now for anything, but it made me feel better when I walked into that schoolhouse."

"Did you like being a teacher?" Angela asked.

"I loved it," said Mama. "I taught for three years and planned to go to the normal school to get proper training but then I met James. I knew that when I married I couldn't teach anyway, so I never did go on."

Miss Barnett and Mama went on talking but Josie wasn't listening. She was trying to imagine an eighteen-year-old Mama teaching and a twenty-one-year-old Mama deciding not to go on to college.

Suddenly she asked, "Why couldn't you teach if you were married?"

Everyone stopped talking. Mama frowned. Josie realized she had interrupted. "Excuse me," she mumbled.

"Well, it's a good question," said Miss Barnett. "Many people believe strongly that a married woman should give all her time to home and family. And that her husband should take care of earning a living, though I notice most wives work just as hard as their husbands with no choice of the kind of work they do."

"That's not all," said Mama. "There are rules that say that a married woman cannot teach. There was such a rule in Iowa then and there's one in Alberta now. That's just the way it is. At the time I got married it seemed quite natural. Now I'm not so sure."

"Could you be married and be an astronomer?" Matt asked Angela.

"I never thought about it," said Angela. "Maybe I would have trouble getting a job at a university. But I can't worry about that now. I just want to start my studies. So I have to teach, at least for six weeks. I suppose I'll survive."

"You will," said Mama. "Bruckner School is brand new. We own a section of land out there so we heard all about the plan to build the school. I understand it has an organ in it because it's used as a church on Sundays."

"That's wonderful," said Angela. "It will make teaching music easier and more fun, too." She paused and frowned a little. "I don't think Mr. Myers, the head of the school board, has very high hopes of me. He's very concerned about discipline and he wanted a male teacher. But he couldn't find one for this term so he had to settle for me."

"You'll do fine," said Mama. "After all, your sister can give you the best possible advice. And you're welcome here any time if I can help." She looked at Matt, who was trying not to stare at the cookies. "Now, Josie, get the tea kettle. I think it's time for refreshments."

FOUR

On the first day of school Josie said to Sam, "I'm going to leave early so that I can stop by for Margaret. I feel kind of bad that I haven't gone to see the Grahams but I wasn't really sure that they wanted me to. Now they might think I'm just unfriendly."

"They were probably too busy to do much visiting," said Sam. "Anyway, Margaret will be glad to have company going to school today."

"Maybe she's forgotten that I promised to come," worried Josie. "I'd better get going."

As Ginger trotted along the familiar track, Josie thought about what it would be like to have a nearby friend. She had imagined it so often, but now that it might really happen her mind was strangely empty of pictures. "We can have picnics," she told herself, "and go out to pick crocuses in the spring and help each other with our work the way Sam and Gregor do sometimes. And we can do homework together." Josie realized she was talking out loud to Ginger, something she only did when she was nervous. Before a recitation day at school, for instance. So why was she nervous now?

"I ought to be happy," she said. "But of course I don't know for sure that Margaret wants a friend. Maybe she'll be perfectly happy all on her own.

Maybe that's why I'm riding along talking to my pony." Josie laughed and then sighed. She couldn't quite imagine laughing with Margaret. She looked so serious.

To distract herself Josie raised her eyes from Ginger's neck to the familiar prairie landscape. It was going to be a hot day. Already the air shimmered a little, but there was a fresh breeze coming from the west. She always liked to think that the west wind came straight from the cool tops of the Rocky Mountains, though sometimes it felt more as if it came from the Sahara Desert. Luckily the school had big windows, and Miss Barnett always opened them wide on hot days.

Thinking of Miss Barnett took Josie's thoughts straight to Angela Barnett. She would be starting at Bruckner School today. Josie hoped she wasn't too scared. She was sure that the pupils would like Angela if she would just smile at them. And if she didn't let the big boys push the little kids around in the schoolyard. That was one thing Miss Barnett never tolerated.

She suddenly noticed that Ginger, who knew the way to school very well, was trotting right past the branch in the trail that led to the Grahams' place.

"Whoa, Ginger," she said. "We're taking a side trip today." She pulled on the reins and guided the pony down the narrower track. The Grahams' place was about two miles farther on but Josie wasn't worried. She had plenty of time. She saw the soddy from far away. It stood alone except for a small sod barn and a fenced farmyard. It was smaller than the Ferriers' wooden house, probably just about the size of their big front room. No doubt Margaret had to sleep in the kitchen. Josie knew what that was like.

As she got closer, she decided that the soddy had a comfortable look. The roof was covered in fresh sod, and there were some black-eyed Susans growing by the door. Mrs. Wilks must have planted them before she left.

Josie had to dismount in order to open the farm-yard gate. Just as she stepped inside, the door of the house opened and Margaret came out. She closed the door carefully behind her before she spoke to Josie. She was wearing a navy blue skirt and a white blouse. Her brown boots were shiny.

"Good morning," she said. "I've been hoping you wouldn't forget to come for me."

"I wouldn't forget," said Josie. "I remember my first day at school here. It was the day the school opened so we all felt shy. We stood around and didn't say anything till little Marcus Leeman said he was scared of school and began to cry. If you remind him about that now he thumps you and he's not little any more."

Margaret looked thoughtful. "I suppose I am a little nervous. I haven't seen a single person except Mother and Father since the day we met you. I tried to imagine the wide open spaces of Canada before we came, but I didn't expect that there would be no people."

"I know," said Josie. "When we first came there was only one house between our place and town. I couldn't believe it. Of course, I do have two brothers. But in the three years we've lived here there hasn't been one girl my age anywhere in the district. Every

time a new girl comes to school she's either a baby or just about to graduate. Well, there was one, but she lived clear on the other side of Curlew, and her family moved into another district in one year. I hope you don't move away in one year." She meant to make a joke, but Margaret answered very seriously.

"I don't think we can," she said. "We have no money left. So don't worry."

Josie knew that was not a joke so she said quickly, "We really should go. Do you want to say goodbye to your parents?"

Margaret frowned a little. "Father is out in the field," she said. "And I've said goodbye to Mother."

"All right," said Josie. "I'll give you a hand up." She put her arms over Ginger's wide back and pulled herself up. Then she reached a hand down to Margaret and pulled her up to sit behind her. "I used to have to climb a fence to mount even a pony like Ginger. I'm glad I finally have longer legs."

She could feel Margaret's fingers digging into her waist and asked, "Have you ridden before?"

"Only a very little. On the ponies at the August fair in our village."

"So you didn't live on a farm?"

"No. My father worked on an estate so he knows farming. At least English farming. But we lived in the village. Then the estate was sold and his job was gone. That's why we came to Canada. Why did you come?"

"The farm in Iowa wasn't big enough to support our family and my uncle's family. My pa was the one with wanderfoot, so he sold Uncle Richard his share of the farm and we came to Alberta."

"I guess I'm the one in my family with wander-foot," said Margaret. "Father just wants his own piece of land, but I don't want to stop here forever. I want to see the mountains and the Pacific Ocean, at least."

"What about your mother?" asked Josie. She had a feeling she shouldn't be asking but she remembered Mrs. Graham's dark, sad eyes and had to know something about her.

Margaret was quiet for a long moment. Then she said, "She hates the prairie. She doesn't say so but I know."

"Didn't she want to come?" asked Josie.

"She said it was her duty," said Margaret. "That's all she ever said about coming to Canada. I know she didn't want to leave the village and her sisters."

"My mother has sisters, too, back in Iowa," said Josie. "She just told me the other day how much she misses them. And she didn't like the prairie when we first came. But I didn't know."

Behind her Margaret was silent. Josie guessed they had talked about mothers long enough but she couldn't think of what to say next. Margaret's quietness seemed to stop her usual chatter.

Ginger went on trotting at her favorite no-nonsense pace. She never liked to hurry but she wanted to reach the school where she could rest and eat grass.

After a while Margaret spoke. "Could you tell me a bit about the school? I suppose I'll be in the upper school, but is it in the same building as the lower school?"

Josie laughed. "There's just one Curlew School and one teacher, Miss Barnett. She teaches everybody,

from six-year-olds to students like Sam who are pre-
paring for college. They say there will be high school
in Curlew soon. If we're lucky it will be there in time
for us."

"But what about your brother? Will he go straight
from Curlew School to a university?"

"Maybe not," said Josie. "Maybe he'll have to go
to Edmonton next year."

"Do they have boarding schools in Edmonton?"
asked Margaret.

"I think he would board with some people and go
to a regular high school." As she said this Josie felt
hollow inside. For the first time she really thought of
Sam gone. "But it's next year he'd go away," she added
more loudly than she intended. "He's only fourteen
now."

Just then Ginger stopped. They had arrived at the
silver house. Josie felt she had to explain. "I like to
look at this house," she said. "So Ginger and I usually stop for a little rest right here."

"It's pretty," said Margaret rather doubtfully.

"It's more like the houses I remember in Iowa than
any other house around here," said Josie. "They have
peaked roofs, too, and porches and fancy trimming.
But most of them were painted white. This one has
never been painted. I call it the silver house. I don't
suppose it's like an English house."

"No," said Margaret. "Where we come from all
the houses are stone. Ours was in a whole row of little houses, all alike. That house is so alone."

"It is a lonely house," said Josie. As they rode on,
she told Margaret its story until she got to the

moment when Mr. McLeod's bride looked at the prairie around the brand-new house. Then she suddenly thought of Margaret's mother and paused.

"What happened then?" asked Margaret. "Didn't she like the house?"

"I don't know," said Josie. "She ended up going back to Ontario but no one knows exactly why. Maybe she just decided she didn't want to get married. Mr. McLeod never moved into the house. He lives in a rooming house in town and the silver house is empty."

"It's too bad," said Margaret. "My father noticed it. A good house going to waste. That's what he said."

FIVE

It seemed to Josie that Margaret slipped into place in Curlew School without changing anything at all. She answered the usual questions politely, but she never said more than was necessary. Even though she was well up to standard on all her lessons, she spent recesses and lunch hours reading. "I must catch up," she insisted.

Miss Barnett said, "I think you need some fresh air, Margaret. Go out and play with the other children." But Margaret simply took her book outside and sat cross-legged on the shady side of the school and went on reading. Even Miss Barnett couldn't get past her polite quietness.

For the first week of school, Josie went every day to the Grahams' house, and every day Margaret was waiting on the doorstep, ready to climb up behind Josie. She was getting the feel of riding on Ginger. Her fingers no longer dug into Josie's waist and she moved naturally to the pony's rhythm instead of sitting stiffly.

But the conversation was stiff. After the two girls spoke of the weather and lessons, silence stretched between them. Margaret seemed to want the silence but Josie's mind bubbled with things she wanted to say. Sometimes they just burst out.

"I can't decide whether the new curtains for my room should be blue or green," she said one day. She was just starting to describe the two fabrics she had seen at Pratt's when Margaret said, "Either would be nice," in such an uninterested voice that Josie couldn't go on. Of course, Margaret had no need for bedroom curtains. Maybe she shouldn't have said anything.

She tried talking about the news from Curlew. "Sam went to the station on Saturday," she said another day. "There was a whole company of soldiers home from France on the train. They said that the war shouldn't last much longer. But I guess you know much more about the war than I do. You lived so close to it."

There was a long silence. At last Margaret said, "Of course there were a great many men who went from our village. It was quite dreadful."

Josie said, "It must have been." Then she couldn't think of another thing to say and the conversation ended.

The next day Josie made up her mind that she was going to talk even if Margaret did not, so she told her all about the baby turkeys. "One of the bachelor settlers decided to go into turkey farming but he just didn't get along with turkeys," she said. "He says they are stupid and stubborn and they turn up their toes and die if a cold wind blows, so he decided to go to British Columbia and grow fruit. At least fruit trees won't run around and squawk idiotically. That's what he says. So he gave us his last twelve baby turkeys. Sam's looking after them, thank goodness. They are stupid. But think of Christmas dinner!"

Again she felt her words fall like stones. Margaret said nothing and Josie thought, "Is she thinking about Christmas dinner in England and how lonely it will be here?" And she, too, was silent for the rest of the ride.

On the Friday of the second week of school Margaret slid off Ginger's back as usual but she didn't open the gate right away. Instead she turned back to Josie and said, "I appreciate that you take me to school and home again every day. With only one horse and my father so busy I don't know what I would do without you. But I've been thinking," she went on. "After this I'll meet you at the fork in the track in the mornings. I think the walk will help. Is that all right?"

"Yes, of course," said Josie. "I'll see you there on Monday then."

As she rode off toward home she puzzled over what Margaret had said. "A two-mile walk will help? What does that mean?" she said to Ginger, who simply twitched her ears.

When she got home Mama was peeling potatoes for supper. Josie put down her school bag and sat at the table watching her.

"You're quiet," said Mama. "All talked out?"

"No," said Josie. "I can't talk to Margaret. I don't know why. I mean, I can talk but she doesn't and so I stop, too. I don't know what to do about it."

"It could be that she doesn't feel comfortable with new people so easily. Or maybe it's too many new things all at once."

"Maybe," said Josie, but she didn't think so.

On Saturday Gregor came by. He joined the Ferriers at the round kitchen table as they finished their breakfast porridge. He and Sam were going to help build a barn for a new settler.

"Have some tea, Gregor," said Mama and poured him a cup. "How is your family?"

"They're fine," said Gregor. "And I have good news. My little sisters, Maria and Katya, they will be going to school starting on Monday."

"That's wonderful," said Mama, and everyone nodded, thinking of Gregor's father. For three years Mr. Chomyk had declared firmly that his daughters were needed to help at home and had no need for Canadian schooling.

It was Josie who asked, "What about your father? Why did he change his mind?"

"You see, my father had to decide whether to go and join the Ukrainian settlement nearer to Edmonton or stay here on the land he chose. He is a stubborn man, my father. He must do things his own way. He will not move to join the settlement. But now he sees that his children must be able to work here. So they must go to school. Also, I'm glad to say that he is proud that his girls already know some English. I have taught them. So now they will go to school."

On Monday, Margaret was waiting at the fork in the trail, just as she had promised. Josie had decided to tell her all about the Chomyks and, for once, Margaret seemed really interested.

"They haven't been to school at all?" she asked. "How old are they?"

"I think that Maria is eight or maybe nine and Katya is seven."

"And they don't hear English at home?"

"Only from Gregor. His English is really good. Sam taught him at first because he couldn't come to school and Sam really wanted to be able to talk to him. We all helped, I guess, and then Gregor just went out and learned. Some people laughed at him because he made funny mistakes. He never seemed to mind, but he told me one time that he wouldn't let it happen to his sisters. So he's been teaching them."

"People laughed at him?" Margaret's voice was unbelieving.

"Yes, they did," said Josie. "I couldn't believe it either but Pa says that some people are just ignorant and they think anyone who isn't exactly like them is stupid and funny. I've even heard of teachers who strap children who speak Ukrainian at school."

"Miss Barnett wouldn't, would she?"

"Of course not. She just punishes students for breaking the rules or being bullies. And she doesn't strap. She sends you to the cloak room or makes you write lines on the board. It is so boring. But she would never punish anyone for being different. The first year of the school, some children cornered me in the schoolyard and told me I was a Yank coward because the United States wasn't in the war then. I was scared. I didn't know I was a Yank and I was only eight anyway."

"What did Miss Barnett do?"

"Each of those students had to write a report on an American immigrant who had made a contribution to

Canada. And she forbade all name-calling like Yank and Polak and all those words. If anyone says them she always hears. Matt says she has ears like a hawk."

For once Margaret laughed. Josie felt that maybe they had started to be friends, just a little.

Maria and Katya were already at the school when Josie and Margaret arrived. Their hair was tightly braided and they wore dark blue dresses and white aprons. Miss Barnett introduced them to the whole school and added, "I know that every one of you will do your best to make our two new pupils feel at home."

Everyone said, "Yes, Miss Barnett," but when morning recess came, it was Margaret who went straight to the front of the room and led the two little girls out into the schoolyard. She showed them where the outhouse was and where the girls skipped rope and the boys played ball.

Josie watched the three of them sitting on the grass chatting and laughing. She had never seen Margaret looking so happy.

In the afternoon when the younger children were reading aloud in turn for Miss Barnett, Margaret raised her hand. "I've finished my reading," she said. "I could hear Maria and Katya. They might need some extra help."

"I'm sure they would appreciate it," said Miss Barnett. "Thank you, Margaret."

After that Margaret helped the two little girls every day and played with them at recess and ate lunch with them. Josie couldn't seem to keep her eyes from being drawn to the group of three. She felt very left out. Margaret was supposed to be her friend. Now it had all gone wrong.

On the last day of the summer term Margaret said, "I'm going to walk into Curlew after school and get some things at the store. Father will meet me there. So I won't be needing to ride home with you."

"I'll see you when school starts again, then," said Josie. She wasn't sorry to have the journey to herself. It was restful not to have to make conversation or feel awkward being silent. When Ginger stopped at the silver house she felt that it was an old friend she hadn't visited in a long time.

"You wait here," she said to the pony. She climbed down and walked up the rise, where she imagined the path might have been, to the front steps of the house. Up close she could see how weathered the wood was, but it looked soft and velvety rather than rough and splintered. It was surprising how much of a view the little rise allowed. It seemed that she could see for miles.

Someone was coming along the track from the direction of town and in a minute she saw it was Sam. She watched him come nearer and wondered whether he would stop or just ride on past. Suddenly she hoped very much that he would stop.

She saw him check King when he came upon Ginger standing riderless. Then his eyes moved up toward the house and he waved to Josie. He left King beside Ginger and came running up the path.

"What are you doing up here?" he said. "I've never seen you go up to the house before."

"I've always thought maybe I shouldn't come up

here. It is somebody's house after all," said Josie. "But today it looked like a good place to sit and think. Mr. McLeod will never know."

Sam didn't say anything. He just sat down on the top step and waited quietly. Josie didn't feel anxious the way she did when Margaret didn't answer. Sam knew her, that was all. He knew that he wouldn't have long to wait before she told him more.

"It's Margaret," she said. "She won't be friends with me. She just won't and then she plays and laughs with Katya and Maria. Why?"

"She doesn't look happy most of the time," said Sam. "Maybe the little girls let her forget about whatever makes her sad. They probably don't even notice. But you do and she knows you might ask her questions any time. Maybe she's afraid of that."

"Afraid?" said Josie. "But I would only want to help."

"She might not want help," said Sam. "Like Mr. Chomyk. He wanted to do everything himself. Now he sees that people can help sometimes. Maybe Margaret will see that after a while."

"I wanted to be friends," said Josie sadly.

"Well, that can mean a lot of things," said Sam. "Look at Gregor and me. I guess we both wanted to be friends, but we didn't know the same language and his life was so different from mine. It took a lot of time for us to get to know each other."

"I guess you're right," said Josie. "Maybe someday I'll get to know Margaret. Anyway, I've managed without a friend for three years now. I should be used to it."

"Don't forget you always have me," said Sam, and he grinned at her. Then he tapped her on the shoulder. "Race you to the horses!"

SIX

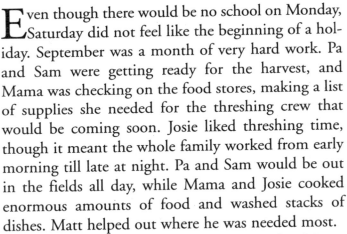

Even though there would be no school on Monday, Saturday did not feel like the beginning of a holiday. September was a month of very hard work. Pa and Sam were getting ready for the harvest, and Mama was checking on the food stores, making a list of supplies she needed for the threshing crew that would be coming soon. Josie liked threshing time, though it meant the whole family worked from early morning till late at night. Pa and Sam would be out in the fields all day, while Mama and Josie cooked enormous amounts of food and washed stacks of dishes. Matt helped out where he was needed most.

Josie looked forward to the excitement, but Mama did not. She got the least sleep of all since she had to get up long before daybreak to get the bread into the oven. While it was baking she roused Josie, and together they started making pancakes and sausages to be ready when the men came in for breakfast.

"We'll need flour, enough to make a dozen loaves a day for four days." Mama stopped and shook her head, thinking of all that baking. "And oatmeal." She went on making the list.

Before she had finished, there was a knock at the door. Josie was surprised to find Angela Barnett standing on the doorstep.

"Come in," she said. "We want to hear about Bruckner School. How was...?" Her voice trailed off. Angela looked very upset.

"Oh, Josie," she said. "I have such an awful problem. I need to talk to your mother about it."

Mama looked up from her list. "Why, Angela, whatever is the matter? Did something go wrong at the school?"

"Not with the children," said Angela. "We got along well. The organ was a help. They loved to sing and they did their lessons promptly for the treat of a singing session. My problem is that Mr. Myers says the school board can't pay me. They have no money."

"No money?" said Mama. "Then why did they hire you?"

"That's what I asked," said Angela. "But Mr. Myers said that it had to do with taxes and I wouldn't understand." She made her face very stern and spoke in a deep voice. "'You've no use for such a sum, young woman. It's good experience you've gotten and I suppose the children have enjoyed their little summer pleasure, singing and playing games.' Singing and playing games! He thinks I taught them nothing. He wouldn't even look at their writing and arithmetic."

Mama turned her shopping list face down and laid her pen beside it, nice and straight. She looked at Angela. "Do you have a contract?" she asked.

"I have a letter signed by Mr. Myers offering me the job at $250."

"And you taught every day and kept order."

"I did, but I think Mr. Myers wants military discipline. I don't believe in that and the children don't

57

need it. They like coming to school. One boy bullied the little children in the schoolyard so I brought him up to the front to sit with the little ones until he could behave like an older student. It didn't take long for him to come around, but Mr. Myers thought he should be strapped. Well, I'm not strapping children for any amount of money."

"You were hired to be a teacher and you taught," said Mama. "Now wash your face and comb your hair. We're going to see Mr. Myers. Josie, you go and fetch Sam and then put on your good blue dress. I want you to come along."

By the time Josie had located Sam, Mama had changed into her best summer dress of dark-green poplin with a small pattern of deep-pink flowers.

"Sam," she said, "I want you to go to town and lay in supplies for the threshers. I've started a list but I can't finish it now. Use your good judgment and take Matt with you. Your father won't be back till afternoon."

Josie stood and stared. She had never seen Mama like this. Her cheeks were pink and her voice was the kind you couldn't argue with. Josie didn't want to argue. She went into her bedroom and quickly changed into her good blue dress. She also spat on the toes of her boots and rubbed them with an old handkerchief so that they shone a little.

When she came back into the kitchen, Mama looked critically at her and then at Angela. "You both look very nice," she said. "But, Angela, you need a hat. I'm afraid it will have to be one of mine."

She disappeared into the bedroom and came back

with a flat straw hat with a black-and-white polka-dotted ribbon around the crown. She held it up and looked at it critically. "It's not going to make the fashion page of the *Bulletin*," she said, "but I've noticed that men listen more respectfully to a woman when she's wearing a hat. Don't ask me why."

She set the hat on Angela's shining red hair and tilted it a little to one side. "You look like a serious young woman," she said. "Come along."

The three of them didn't talk on the way to Mr. Myers' place. Mama drove the buggy along the rutted track much faster than usual. Josie saw her lips move now and then as if she was rehearsing a speech. Angela looked a little stunned but hopeful.

The Myers' farm was like most in the district. It had a small wooden house, a barn and a few sheds. But the barn was larger than most and the house was freshly painted.

Mr. Myers was working in the barn but he came out when he heard the sound of the gate being opened. He helped Mama unhitch Lady and led the horse over to the watering trough. Then he looked from Mama to Angela and back again.

"I have a matter to discuss with you," said Mama. "It won't take long but I'd prefer not to stand in the hot sun."

"Come into the house then," said Mr. Myers. "But if this has to do with Miss Barnett here, I don't know what we can talk about. This is Bruckner district and you live in Curlew district."

Mama didn't answer until they were inside. Josie was surprised to find that instead of one big front room, this house had a tiny central hall with doors on either side. To the left must be the kitchen, she thought, judging from the rattling of pots and pans. It was getting near to dinner time.

Mr. Myers opened the door to the right and ushered them into a small parlor furnished with two horsehair settees and a large carved rocker.

Mama gestured to Josie and Angela to sit down. She remained standing, facing Mr. Myers.

"What is this about, Mrs. Ferrier?" he said impatiently.

"Angela Barnett has informed me that although she has satisfactorily completed teaching the summer term at Bruckner School, you do not intend to pay her. I find that very surprising."

"I have explained to Miss Barnett that we don't have sufficient funds to pay her," said Mr. Myers. "It is true that we offered $250 for the term, thinking that we would get an experienced male teacher who would maintain discipline. A young girl like Miss Barnett is hardly worth so much and the taxes have been slow to come in. And again I must ask you, what business is this of yours, Mrs. Ferrier?"

"To begin with it's my business because the education of the children of this whole region is important to me. If school districts in the Curlew area get the reputation of failing to live up to their agreements, no good teacher, male or female, will want to come here."

"By fall when the real teacher comes, we will be in good shape to pay him," said Mr. Myers. "Miss Barnett will go on with her life, probably get married and have children soon. Then she will know how important discipline is if children are to learn in an orderly fashion."

Angela stood up. "Mr. Myers," she said. "I kept order. The children learned. I ask that you look at their copy books. Look at the children, for that matter. They were pleased to come to school and they worked hard. And so did I."

"I'm sorry, Miss Barnett. I cannot pay you. That is my final word." Josie noticed that Mr. Myers was getting a little red in the face, and his voice was rising.

Mama said quickly, "From that I conclude that, if you could pay Miss Barnett, you would. Well, Mr. Myers, I may not live in Bruckner district, but my husband and I own land here, and I happen to know that we paid our annual tax on that land only two days ago. Perhaps that has not come to your attention. Perhaps you have not had time to open the envelope. I am sure that your coffers were not entirely empty before our payment arrived. Now there will surely be enough to pay Miss Barnett."

Mr. Myers stared at Mama. Mama looked him straight in the eye and smiled. "I'm sure you will be relieved to pay Miss Barnett. She does have a letter of agreement from you and she is most determined to have the money to attend university. It would be difficult for her to have to wait while lawyers argued the case."

The school board chairman opened his mouth and shut it again. Then, without saying anything, he left the room. Josie could hear voices in the kitchen, then the sound of a door shutting, perhaps a little harder than necessary.

In a few minutes he was back in the parlor with an envelope in his hand. He handed it to Angela. "This is your pay, in full," he said. "It turned out that my wife had put the Ferriers' payment aside and forgotten to give it to me." He did not look at Mama. "I hope that you and your friends will be satisfied now and that you will find work that is suitable."

"Thank you, Mr. Myers," said Angela. "I intend to be an astronomer."

"Good day," said Mama, and she led Josie and Angela out of the house.

When they were a good way down the road, Mama let Lady slow to a walk. "The pity is," she said, "as long as that man is head of the school board, they will probably not hire one young woman to teach. Oh, well, we won today."

"Yes," said Angela, "because you were magnificent. Thank you with all my heart, for the money and for showing me that there are ways to stand up for yourself. I'll remember always."

"I'll remember, too," said Josie.

Mama smiled. "It was lucky that I remembered about those taxes." She bit her lip thoughtfully. "You know," she finally said, "all this excitement makes me think about how I spend my own time. Surely there are more important things to do than get up at three in the morning to make bread. I have enough money on hand to buy bread from the baker for the threshing crew and I will."

"What will people say?" asked Josie. She knew that people set great store by all the homemade food farm wives provided for the threshers.

"They'll say I'm a sorry excuse for a farm wife," said Mama. "Just like Mr. Myers said that Angela wasn't a good teacher because she didn't teach his way. Well, she's a good teacher and I'm a good farm wife. So that's all there is to say about that."

She flicked the reins. Lady picked up her pace and they laughed and talked all the way home.

When Pa got home they told him all about Angela and Mr. Myers. Mama's eyes were still full of excitement, but Pa rubbed his forehead and said, "I'm glad that you got that young woman what was rightfully hers, but I hope it doesn't cause bad feeling."

"Angela will be off in Edmonton," said Mama, "so I suppose you mean bad feeling against me and also you for having such a bold wife. I thought about that, James, but it was a situation of right and wrong. People must be paid fairly for what they do and not be judged as not up to standard simply because they are women."

"That's true enough," said Pa. "Myers hired a woman and he has to be prepared to pay her. I guess people like him are having a hard time accepting all the things women are doing these days."

"It's like a wall," thought Josie. "Mr. Myers thinks there is a wall between what men can do and women can do." It suddenly struck her that it was funny that Angela wanted to be an astronomer and Katherine Stinson wanted to be an aviator. They were determined to get over that wall. Even the sky was not too high for them. The thought made her laugh a little, and Mama and Pa were suddenly looking at her.

"What about it, Josie?" said Pa. "Would our friend Myers approve of your ambitions?"

"I don't know yet," said Josie. "But I want Mama on my side. She was magnificent, Pa. Angela said so. And Mama decided something, too. About her own work, I mean."

"Oh, yes," said Mama. "Sit down, James. Let me tell you about bread baking."

SEVEN

On the first day of the fall school term Margaret was waiting by the trail in her usual spot. She waved when she saw Josie coming.

"I'm glad school is starting again," she said, once she was up on Ginger's back. "I didn't have much to do during the holiday."

"Did your father have crops to bring in?" asked Josie, just to keep the conversation going. She already knew the answer. Pa had checked with Mr. Graham to see if he needed any help.

"Not really," said Margaret. "I guess Mr. Wilks knew they were moving and didn't put in many crops. But we planned for that," she added hastily. "We have enough food to last us through the winter, I'm quite sure."

Josie hoped so. She was always surprised how the supplies that filled their cellar at the beginning of winter just melted away while everything else was frozen solid. It would do no good to worry Margaret, though, so she said nothing.

She was so used to the silence of their rides together that she was startled when Margaret suddenly said, "I walked to the silver house twice last week."

"By yourself?" asked Josie sharply. She could just see the house coming into view and she suddenly felt unreasonably worried that it would have changed.

"Well, yes," said Margaret. "Of course."

Josie shook herself a little. What was she so cranky about? "What did you do there?" she said more peacefully.

"Nothing," said Margaret. "I just walked around the outside and tried to imagine a garden in front of it. Blue delphiniums by the steps, and daisies. I suppose roses would just die."

"There are wild roses on the prairie," said Josie. "They look kind of plain compared to garden roses but I love them. They're deep pink with golden centers."

"They sound beautiful," said Margaret. "In England we had red roses in our garden. My mother used to say a garden isn't a garden without roses. I don't think she would care for wild roses though."

She was quiet for a minute. Ginger had come to her usual stop and both girls looked up at the little house.

"Don't you wonder what's inside?" Margaret asked. "Do you think we could look in the windows?"

"I suppose we could," said Josie. "I never have because I like to think of it all cozy and polished and I know that really it will be empty and dusty. But we could go up on the porch one day and look in."

"I suppose it would be locked," said Margaret.

"I don't know," said Josie. "Nobody locks their doors around here, but Mr. McLeod might. The house really is his, you know." She didn't want to explain that, in her imagination, it was actually hers. "I don't think we should open the door," she added firmly.

She could feel Margaret sigh before she said, "I know you're right. I just can't stop thinking about it. Maybe it comes from living in a soddy. I get to thinking about proper windows and having my own room."

Josie nudged Ginger and they rode on. Now she was the one who wanted to be quiet. She had to get used to the idea that she was no longer the only one to care about the silver house.

When they reached the schoolyard she didn't mind that Katya and Maria rushed up to Margaret and took her off to play with them. Josie made sure Ginger had a good drink of water and then she went into the school.

Miss Barnett was putting a bunch of goldenrod into a jar of water. "Good morning, Josie," she said. "I have news from Angela. She's all settled in the women's residence at the university. Thanks to your mother, she can pay her tuition and she has a job waiting on tables. The pay will help her with room and board."

"Do you think she really will be an astronomer?" asked Josie.

"She's very determined," said Miss Barnett. "It's not an easy field even for a man to get into and I'm sure that being a woman won't help. But, yes, I think she has a very good chance. At least she'll do something interesting. Of that I am very sure." She picked up the bell that sat on her desk and went out on the doorstep to ring it. The school day had begun.

After attendance was taken and the younger children were busy doing sums in their copy books, Miss

Barnett spoke to the students in the older grades. "I would like each of you to write an essay about a person you admire. It might be someone famous or someone you know. I want detailed information about the person's life and accomplishments and I want to know why you admire him or her. I expect a neat copy with a minimum of ink blots."

Josie made a face. Ink blots were a problem for her because she always got too interested in what she was writing and pressed down too hard. The point of the pen separated, and a dreaded blob of ink slid off the pen onto her carefully written page. She resigned herself to a few more blots than Miss Barnett would like.

The subject of the essay was no problem at all. She would write about Katherine Stinson. She had carefully saved all the newspaper articles she had found. She just hoped they would provide enough information.

After supper that evening, Josie read through the articles and listed every fact she found.

1. Katherine Stinson flew the plane carrying the first air mail from Calgary to Edmonton and delivered the letters at the Edmonton Exhibition July 9, 1918.
2. K.S. is young. (They keep calling her a girl but I don't think she can really be that young. What do they mean by a girl?)
3. She did flying exhibitions in Edmonton and Calgary two years ago. (Maybe she's an American since it never says where in Canada she comes from.)
4. She drives a racing car also.
5. She is brave.
6. She is famous.

Josie looked at her notes and scowled. It wasn't enough. The newspapers were full of words like "plucky" and "daring," but they were short on facts. And where could she get facts? There were no books about Katherine Stinson. Margaret had chosen Florence Nightingale and she had a whole book full of information. And Sam was writing about Gregor. He could talk to him any day.

"If only I could talk to Katherine Stinson," Josie said to Mama, "or write her a letter."

Suddenly she was struck by a brilliant thought. "I will write her a letter—one I would send to her if I could. Maybe Miss Barnett will give me marks for originality." She chewed her pencil for a few minutes and then began to write.

I have chosen to write about the aviator, Katherine Stinson, who carried the first air mail from Calgary to Edmonton. She delivered it to the Edmonton Exhibition this year. She also put on a wonderful demonstration of flying. I admire Katherine Stinson for at least three reasons.

1. She is a great success even though she is very young.

2. She is fearless and is doing things no one else has done.

3. She has to know a lot of different things, for example, how engines work and how to find her way across the land.

All of these things are very inspiring to me because she is a woman and she has given me a new ideal of what women can do.

The problem is that it is very hard to get information

about her. The newspapers don't have very many facts. My wish is that I could write her a letter. If I could do that, maybe I could find out what I need to know. This is what I would say:

Dear Miss Stinson,
My name is Josie Ferrier. I'm eleven years old and I live on a farm near Curlew, Alberta. I read about you in the Edmonton Bulletin. More than anything I wish I had seen you fly when you brought the mail from Calgary to Edmonton but I live too far from Edmonton to come to the exhibition. I have never even seen an airplane. I think you are wonderful to fly one so expertly. There are many questions I would ask you if I could talk to you. I hope you won't mind if I ask you some of them now.

1. What made you want to fly and how did you learn to be an aviator?
2. What do you love most about flying?
3. Are you ever afraid?
4. Will you always fly? Where do you want to fly next?

I don't want to bother you with more questions so I will stop. But I do want to tell you that I am writing an essay about a person I admire and that person is you! I admire you because you are doing a brave and surprising thing. You are a real pioneer. I can't think of a way to be a pioneer myself but I'm going to try.

Thank you for reading my letter. I'll put my address on it just in case you want to answer.
Yours truly,
Josephine Ferrier

When Miss Barnett read Josie's rough copy the next day she said, "That's a very original approach to writing a factual essay, Josie. But even if you got answers to all these questions, you still would not have many facts."

"I know," said Josie. "But some questions are just rude if you put them in a letter. All the newspapers say she is young but I can't ask how old she is, can I?"

"Certainly not," said Miss Barnett. "You need an outside source for that kind of information. But you have written a good letter. I think you should send it."

"But it's an imaginary letter!" said Josie. "I didn't think of really sending it. Besides, I don't have Miss Stinson's address."

"It's a perfectly good letter," said Miss Barnett. "Of course you'll need to make a good copy. And as for where to send it, that will be a test of your ingenuity." She stood up to dismiss the school, and Josie knew she had been given an assignment.

Outside she caught up with Sam. "Could you take Margaret to her turn-off? I want to go into town and talk to Mr. Murray at the newspaper. Tell Mama I won't be long."

The editor of the Curlew *Star* was busy proofreading the copy for Friday's edition.

"What can I do for you, Josie?" he asked.

"It's Katherine Stinson again," said Josie. "I want to send her a letter but I don't even know what city she lives in. And I need some facts about her, too. How do you get information about somebody who is not already in history?"

"The *Bulletin* articles don't help?" asked Mr. Murray.

"They helped some. But mostly they tell about what she did, not about her. And Miss Barnett wants facts."

"Miss Barnett would make a good editor," said Mr. Murray. "The *Bulletin* has some of that information on file, of course. They use it for background. I'll tell you what. You write down about five or six questions and I'll send them to my friend Bill Stevens. He works for the *Bulletin* and I'm sure he'll be glad to send you the facts you need."

"That will be perfect," said Josie. "Thank you very, very much. Can I sit down and do it now?"

"Pull up a chair. There's plenty of paper in that stack. Just remember the five newspaper reporter's questions—Who, What, When, Where and How."

Josie took a pencil out of her school bag. For a few moments she doodled and thought. Then she began to write. It took her just ten minutes to write down her questions quite neatly. Of course with a pencil there was no problem with blots.

1. When did K.S. learn to fly? How old was she then? (I'm sorry if this is a rude question but I really want to know.)
2. Who taught her to fly?
3. Where does she live and where has she flown besides Calgary and Edmonton?
4. What does she do besides flying at exhibitions?
5. How did she get to be famous?

Josie dug her pencil into the dot under the last question mark. Then she said, "Excuse me, Mr. Murray. I've got the five questions for Mr. Stevens but I also want to know why Miss Stinson became an aviator. I think that she's the only one who could answer that."

"That is a problem," said Mr. Murray.

Josie looked at him. He looked sympathetic and interested so she went on. "You see, I've written her a letter. If I could send it to her she might answer. But I don't have her address."

"Well, she certainly can't answer it if you don't send it. Pass it along to Bill. He probably can find an address to send it to. It's worth trying."

"I have to copy the letter in ink," said Josie. "I'll do it tonight and I'll write to Bill, I mean Mr. Stevens, too, so he'll understand. I'll bring everything in tomorrow. Thank you, Mr. Murray."

She found him the next day still working on the paper for the week. He was frowning over one of the headlines on the proof sheet. It had a big red question mark beside it. Josie came around his desk so she wouldn't have to read it upside down.

Influenza Spreads in Alberta.

Mr. Murray looked at it and shook his head.

"Now this is one of the decisions that faces an editor," he said. "How big and black should I make that headline? It's real news, important news. Folks need to know about this sickness, but I don't want to start a panic. You'd be surprised how many people don't pay much attention to the story. They just read the headlines."

"Is the influenza really coming here?"

"Yes. I'm afraid it is. The epidemic has been working its way west since spring. Of course, with the population spread out over the countryside the way it is here, it may not get to so many people. But it's very important for my readers to know it's coming. I'd better go with the big headline."

Josie gave him her envelope and then rode home. She wanted to think about Katherine Stinson, but she kept worrying about the influenza instead. People said that the sickness had come home from the war with the soldiers, but until now it had seemed very far away. Thousands of people in the east had been sick and many had died. Mama's aunt who lived in Philadelphia was one who had died. She was very old and Josie had never met her but she remembered how sad Mama was the day the letter came.

When she got home, Matt was throwing his rubber ball against the side of the barn to the rhythm of a rhyme. It was something about a bird, but Matt was bouncing and chanting so fast that at first Josie couldn't make out the words. When he saw that she was listening he slowed down.

I had a little bird and her name was Enza
I opened up the window and in-flu-ENZA!

He stopped bouncing and said enthusiastically, "Johnny Clarkson taught me that. Do you get it?"

"I get it," said Josie, but she couldn't laugh, not even to please Matt.

EIGHT

On a Monday in early November Sam asked Josie if she would feed the turkeys for him. "I've got to help level the rink so we can put the ice in as soon as it stays cold enough. We want to start playing hockey," he said.

"I'll do it this once," said Josie. "But, remember, the turkeys are yours to take care of. I don't mind chickens but turkeys are just too big to be so foolish."

Feeding the turkeys was certainly not an easy chore. They had developed a habit of rushing toward anyone who came into their pen, so Josie had to brave their pushing and squawking, scoop feed into their pans and get away as fast as possible. By the time she was finished, she quite sympathized with the settler who had given up on the annoying birds.

The extra chore made her late leaving home, so she was very surprised not to find Margaret waiting for her at the fork in the track. Maybe it was so late that she had walked on to school. She certainly wasn't in sight. Josie decided not to wait. She was so sure Margaret was already at school that she was startled to find the seat next to hers empty when she arrived breathlessly during opening exercises.

Miss Barnett saw her surprise and said, "I expect

Margaret will be back tomorrow. If there's something wrong we're sure to hear about it."

Josie knew this was common sense, but she couldn't help worrying. Students were absent from school for all sorts of reasons, but not Margaret. She hadn't missed a day yet, and Josie had the feeling that coming to school was important to her in some special way. It would take something serious to keep her at home.

At noon she said to Sam, "I can't stop wondering why Margaret didn't come to school. Maybe it seems silly but I have to be sure she's all right. Will you and Matt stop by the Grahams' place with me after school?"

"But why do you need us?" Sam was puzzled.

"I just have a bad feeling. Margaret would never miss if something wasn't wrong. They might need some help."

"Well, it won't take long," said Sam. "Probably her folks just needed her to do some work."

"I hope so," said Josie, but all afternoon she kept watching the big clock that hung over Miss Barnett's desk.

When the three Ferriers arrived at the Grahams' place, Josie looked around anxiously. There was no one in the farmyard. The animals were not in sight, and no sound came from the house or barn.

"Look," said Sam, "there's smoke coming from the chimney." His voice was relieved. "Josie, you go and see how Margaret is. Matt and I will wait."

Josie went to the door. She knocked and waited. Then she knocked again. What if no one answered?

But then the door opened slowly, and Margaret stood there, blinking in the afternoon sun.

"Josie," she said, "why are you here? And Sam and Matt. . ." Her voice trailed off.

"We just wanted to make sure you're all right," said Josie. "You didn't come to school so I got a little worried."

Margaret glanced back into the house as if to be sure that she could be gone for a moment. Then she stepped out into the yard and closed the door behind her.

"It's my father," she said. "He has a fever so I had to do the chores and stay with him."

"I guess your mother needed the help." Margaret didn't answer so Josie went on, "Or is she sick, too?"

For a long moment Josie could see that Margaret was trying to make up her mind. At last she bit her lip and said in a flat voice, "Not exactly sick. You might as well come in."

Josie looked over at Sam and Matt. "Don't go away," she said, and she followed Margaret through the door.

It was dark inside the soddy, and at first Josie could only see the shape of the big coal stove that stood in the middle of the room. Then she made out a square table and two chairs. In one corner was a large trunk with boxes stacked on top of it. There were more boxes piled by the door. In the other corner, in front of a curtain that divided the house into two sections, was a rocking chair. In it sat Mrs. Graham. She was wearing a dark dress, and she sat so still that it took Josie a minute to see her.

"Mother," said Margaret, "Josie's here. She came

to see me because I was absent from school today."

Mrs. Graham turned her face toward Josie, but she didn't speak. Then she turned away. Josie began to feel as if she might be invisible. Margaret opened the door again and, taking Josie's arm, pulled her out into the bright sunlight.

"You see how it is," she said in a low voice. "My mother hardly speaks, and she won't unpack the trunk or the boxes. If I open one or Father does she starts to cry. She wants to go back to England. Now Father is sick and she's really scared. So am I and I can't go to school because I have to look after Father and the animals."

"Do you think your father has influenza?" asked Josie bluntly.

Margaret shrugged. "I don't know," she said. "He was very tired last night and went straight to bed after chores. This morning he just couldn't get up. I give him water to drink and I sat with Mother all day. I don't know what else to do."

Sam and Matt had been standing with the horses, listening. Now Sam said, "I'll look after your animals. Matt, you take King and ride home and tell Pa and Mama what's happening. They'll think of something to do."

Margaret hardly seemed to be paying attention. She kept looking toward the house, but she said, "Thank you for doing the chores. I'd better go in and see how my father is." Then she was gone.

Josie followed Sam into the barn. Unlike the house it had a settled-in look with all the implements and tools neatly stored along the walls and the mangers freshly built out of new wood. Sam and Josie cleaned out the stalls and made sure the two cows and the horse and the chickens all had plenty of feed. Then Sam pumped water for the watering trough. Josie searched in the straw of the little loft where the chickens were roosting and found three eggs. When this work was done, they sat on two upturned buckets beside the barn.

"Did you see Mrs. Graham?" asked Sam.

"Yes," said Josie. "She was just sitting in a rocking chair. She didn't say anything. It was as if I wasn't even there."

"It sounds as if she's the one who doesn't want to be here."

"You heard Margaret. Her mother wants to be in England. But she must have known that Alberta wouldn't be like England."

"I think people from other places just can't imagine the prairie," said Sam quietly. "I was surprised myself and Iowa is pretty flat and wide open. And for people who have lived in hill country, I've heard that the space and the loneliness can frighten them."

"Maybe that's why Mr. McLeod's bride left so fast," said Josie. "Well, Mrs. Graham can't leave but she isn't getting settled here either. The house looks like they just came yesterday. There are stacks of boxes that aren't unpacked. It's awful, Sam. Awful for Margaret."

"For all of them, I guess. You can tell that Mr. Graham has been spending a lot of time fixing up the barn, and Margaret goes to school. But they all have to live together in the house. I wonder whether Mrs.

Graham ever goes into town or sees a neighbor."

"I don't think so. I bet she doesn't even open the door when Margaret and Mr. Graham are away. I think she hates the land so much that she's made up her mind to shut herself away from it. She probably doesn't even want to know the people who live here. That's why Margaret walks to the main trail to meet me. I guess it helps her to have some time between her mother and the rest of us. Well, at least now I know what's wrong."

They sat quietly then until Margaret came out of the house. "I think Father is a little better," she said. "He's not so hot. But his sheets are soaked with sweat and I can't find any others."

"I'm sure Mama will come back with Matt. She'll know what to do," said Josie.

Margaret sat down on the dusty ground and covered her face with her hands. After a minute she looked up. "I'm glad you came," she said. "Mother says we shouldn't be beholden to anyone here because then we'll have to help them back and we'll never get away. But we're not going to leave for a long time anyway and we can't live all on our own, especially now that Father is sick. What if he dies?"

The question shocked Josie so much that she put her hand over her mouth to stop herself from gasping. But she had to say something.

"Dies? Is he that sick?"

"I don't know," said Margaret. "But people do die of the influenza. Very strong people. They did at home, in England. I hoped there wouldn't be flu in Canada, but it followed us."

"We'll help you all we can, no matter what happens," said Sam. Josie could feel that he wanted to get up and do something, but he stayed still. Margaret rested her head against her bent knees. After a few minutes Josie thought she might be asleep, but at the faint sound of buggy wheels she sat up straight.

Josie jumped up and looked down the track. "It's Mama, I think," she said. "I don't see Pa."

It was Mama. She climbed down from the buggy and went to Margaret. She didn't hug her but she touched her on the shoulder and said, "You poor child, having to manage by yourself. My husband has gone for the doctor and I've brought you some supper and some clean sheets."

She went into the house, and Margaret and Josie followed. Mrs. Graham still sat in her rocking chair. When she saw Mama she stared for a moment and then very slowly stood up.

"Good afternoon," she said. "I apologize for the disorder of the house. There seems to be no place to put anything and we won't be staying long, I feel sure. So it was hardly worthwhile to unpack."

"Never mind," said Mama. "You're living here for now and I'm sure the girls would like to tidy up a little. I've brought you some supper and the doctor will be coming. For Mr. Graham," she added, as Mrs. Graham seemed about to object.

"How will we pay him?" Mrs. Graham's voice rose. "We have to save every penny until we have enough to go back to England. Our money is gone."

"Dr. Warren will wait for payment," said Mama. "He's a good man. Don't worry. Your husband must see a doctor, otherwise we won't know the best things to do for him. Now, let me make you a cup of tea."

Mrs. Graham sat down. Mama sent Josie to fill the kettle. Then she stirred up the fire and set the kettle and an iron pot of stew on the stove and began to slice bread. When the kettle boiled, she took a little box of tea out of her basket.

"Where is the teapot, dear?" she said to Margaret.

"It's still in a box. I know just where it is. The everyday teapot, I mean." She looked at her mother and waited.

"You would like a cup of tea, wouldn't you?" said Mama. Mrs. Graham nodded slowly. "We'll need the teapot then." Mama smiled at Margaret. "I'm glad you know where it is."

Margaret went to one of the large wooden boxes that sat near the door. The top had been pried off but the box was still full of objects wrapped in packing paper.

"There are more dishes in here," Margaret told Josie. "And a tablecloth and some aprons. I remember packing kitchen things all together."

"Do you have a place to put them?" asked Josie.

"Father built some shelves."

Josie looked where she pointed and saw that a sturdy set of shelves stood against the wall. She hadn't noticed them because they were empty. She and Margaret began to lift the dishes out of the box, unwrap them and set them on the shelves. They were white with two bands of blue around the edges.

"What have you been eating from?" Josie asked.

"The tin plates we had on the journey. And the tin cups. It's as if the journey has never ended."

"The dishes make the room look brighter already," said Mama, "and I think that big parcel must be the teapot." She took it and rinsed it with boiling water, then put in the tea and more boiling water. When it had steeped for five minutes, she poured Mrs. Graham a cup.

"I hope you'll approve of this tea," she said. "Our English neighbors, the Martingales, taught me the proper English way to make it."

Mrs. Graham took the cup. For several moments she simply held it carefully balanced on its saucer. Then she took a sip. "It's very good," she said. Then, in a rush, "You are very kind." She lowered her eyes and slowly drank her tea.

"Now I had better see how Mr. Graham is doing. Margaret, you've been taking care of your father, haven't you? So you'll come in and help me change the sheets. Josie, I want you and Sam to go on home. I'll wait for Dr. Warren. There's no use you getting more exposed than you must."

Josie and Sam rode home together on Ginger. "How are things in the house?" Sam asked.

"I don't know how Mr. Graham is, but Mrs. Graham drank a cup of tea and Margaret and I unpacked some dishes. Sam, I thought Mama would just go in and get everything straightened out, but nothing has really changed."

"How could she? It's not so simple to straighten everything out for people."

"I know. She can't make Mrs. Graham happy about the prairies. It's just that I hate to think of Margaret in that dismal house."

"It explains why she's always been so quiet. She didn't want you to know what was wrong."

"I guess you're right. When you have a secret you have to be quiet or you might tell. Now maybe we can just talk because we want to talk. Maybe we'll even be friends."

Pa and Matt were at home when they arrived. "We found the doctor," said Matt. "We were lucky. He's a very busy man, he says."

"Yes," said Pa. "The influenza is spreading. They're talking about closing the railroad stations in the smaller towns like Curlew to try to keep it under control, but it seems that it's already here."

Josie and Sam got some supper together. Sam found the pot of stew Mama had left in the cool cellar, and there was a cabbage saved from the garden. Josie made cole slaw. They waited for Mama till it was dark. Then just as they were about to sit down, she came home.

"I waited for Dr. Warren," she said. "He says that Mr. Graham is probably over the worst. Margaret did a very good job. But now he must rest till the fever is completely gone. I said that Sam and Matt would stop and do the chores morning and night, and I'll bring food and clean laundry. I think Mrs. Graham will stir herself a little, at least. She has pride but, poor woman, she seems to be in a daze. Margaret will have to miss some more school, I'm afraid."

"All the children will," said Pa. "The school will be closed after tomorrow until this epidemic has passed. The school board decided that one more day wouldn't increase the danger, and that way you'll have your books and assignments to work on."

For a moment all the Ferriers sat quietly and looked at each other. Then Pa said, "We're all healthy now and I pray that we stay that way. And we have a good meal before us." They picked up their forks. The stew was delicious.

NINE

The next day seemed strangely warm and still. The sky was a cool early-winter blue and the only clouds lay in a thin line along the western horizon. There was no wind to stir the grass as Josie and Sam and Matt rode to school. Even the gophers sat motionless, and the hawks seemed to hang in the air without moving their wings.

School was strange, too. The children played in the schoolyard and recited their lessons, but everyone was quieter and politer than usual. Josie found herself looking at people as if she might not see them again for a very long time.

Miss Barnett felt the solemn mood. "It feels like the *Titanic* after the iceberg hit," she said to some of the older students when she went out at lunch hour and found them sitting on the steps talking quietly. "Closing the school is a wise precaution, but we'll be seeing each other soon, I promise you." She began to ring the bell vigorously.

Instead of going on with lessons in the afternoon, Miss Barnett announced a spelling bee. "To challenge you while you have this school break I'm going to write on the board every word that is missed. I want you to copy them down and study them and when we're back together we'll have a rematch. I hope that every one of you will know one hundred percent of these words by heart."

Josie groaned inwardly. She would never get one hundred percent right on a spelling test. She loved to write but spelling was just like ink blots. It slowed her down. Spelling bees were fun, though. She was glad to see Matt lining up on her side of the room. He was one of the best spellers in the school, even though he was only nine.

Today he was one of the last three students left standing. The other two would have been in high school if there had been one. It was the word propinquity that tripped him up. He put a *g* in it, but he sat down looking pleased with himself.

After everyone had copied down the missed words, Miss Barnett gave each class special assignments to do at home while the school was closed. When they had all shut their copy books and put their pencils in their pencil cases, she stood in front of her desk and spoke to the whole school.

"We don't know how long the school will be closed," she said. "I think it is very possible that it won't reopen before Christmas, so we may not see each other again until spring term. That may seem far away, but I hope you will take some time each day to do the lessons I have set you. That way we won't be so far behind when school takes up again." Miss Barnett turned to the shelf of books behind her desk. "I hope you will read, too. Reading is one of the best ways to pass time, have fun, and learn new things. If any of you would like to borrow one of my books to take home, please come to the front of the room."

Josie was on her feet immediately. She knew which book she wanted. She had read and loved *Little Women* and *Good Wives* by Louisa May Alcott. Now she had her eye on Miss Barnett's copy of *Eight Cousins*.

"Could I take one for Margaret, too?"

"Of course," said Miss Barnett. "Take *The Secret Garden*. It's about a girl who has to come to a place that's very strange to her. I think Margaret would like it."

Josie looked at Miss Barnett in surprise. How could she know so much about how Margaret felt? But Miss Barnett was busy giving Sam a book on King Arthur and helping Matt choose Andrew Lang's *Book of Animal Stories*. Then she waited until everyone was seated again and said, "Now, children, it's dismissal time. I'll miss you and I hope we'll be together again soon."

"Goodbye, Miss Barnett," they all said in chorus, just as if it were any other day. But there was none of the usual surreptitious shoving and whispering as the children gathered up their books and coats and went out into the sunshine.

In spite of everything, Josie couldn't help having a bit of a holiday feeling. The heavy books in her school bag were part of the reason. "Holiday reading." She had read about that somewhere. Now she had some holiday reading herself.

Sam and Matt stayed behind to help Miss Barnett close up the school, so Josie rode on alone. The golden stillness of the morning still lay over the prairie, and she jumped when she heard a voice calling, "Josie! Josie! Stop!"

She looked up and realized she had almost come to the silver house. And there was Margaret standing on the porch, waving at her.

"Josie, do come up," she called.

Josie left Ginger by the track and walked up the slope to the silver house.

Margaret watched her impatiently. "I hoped I would catch you," she said. "I could only come away for a little while."

"How is your father?" asked Josie.

"He's very weak and a little feverish but he's still getting better. Dr. Warren told Mother it's very, very important to keep him in bed, so she moved her chair into the bedroom where she could watch over him. And she told me to unpack the bedding. I think she felt a little embarrassed that we had to use your sheets."

Josie thought that Margaret herself looked a little feverish. Not sick but excited, as if her energy was bursting out instead of being kept inside. She looked at Josie intently and said, "I really want to look in the windows. I waited for you because I didn't think it was fair to do it without you. It won't do any harm."

"I know," said Josie. She still felt strange about peering in those dusty windows, but there was no one in the silver house to care. Anyway, she certainly wasn't going to let Margaret do it on her own.

They both turned around and looked at the front of the house, just as if they had come up a front path intending to make a call.

There were two windows that opened onto the porch, one on each side of the door. There was a square window in the door, too, divided into small diamond-shaped panes. Without speaking, the girls went to the door first. They stood on tiptoe and through the grimy glass saw a hallway with a staircase leading straight up. At the bottom was a plain, square newel post. There was nothing more to look at, so they moved to the left-hand window. The room inside was perfectly empty. Dust lay thick on the floor.

"You can tell no one's been in there for a long time," said Josie. "There would be footprints."

The room to the right was just as dusty, but it was not empty. There was a black iron heating stove in the corner with two wooden chairs in front of it and a small round table between them. In the middle of the table was a vase holding the dry stems of some long-dead flowers.

"Look," said Margaret. "He put flowers in the vase for her, and she never saw them."

They slowly backed away from the window. Margaret paused for a minute in front of the door. For a moment Josie was afraid she would put her hand on the patterned brass doorknob and try to turn it. What if she opened that door?

But Margaret turned toward the steps and said, "There's a back porch, too, a little one. Let's see if we can look into the kitchen."

The back porch had one window. Through it they could see that the kitchen had a cookstove and a table. An iron pot and a tea kettle sat on the stove and a frying pan hung on the wall, but what Josie and Margaret stared at were the dishes neatly arranged on

a shelf above the table. The plates and bowls were stacked and seemed to be ordinary white dishes, but on the dusty cups the girls could see two bands of blue.

"Look," said Josie. "Aren't they like your dishes?"

"Exactly," said Margaret. "They are exactly the same."

"Maybe it's a common pattern," said Josie.

"Well, I suppose it is," said Margaret. "They are our everyday dishes. But still, it seems so strange." She looked at the dishes for a moment longer. "They're waiting for someone to come and use them. What a pity." She stepped back from the window and turned to look out across the prairie. "I should be getting home," she said. "When I left, Mother was telling Father stories about when they were young. I even heard her laugh once."

"I'm glad," said Josie. "Did Mama come with some food?"

"Yes, and she said she was going on to take some to one of the bachelors who is sick. She said to tell you to start supper because she might be late."

"Well, then, I'd better hurry," said Josie. She jumped down from the porch and began to walk to the front of the house. "Shall I take you to the turn-off?"

"No need," said Margaret. "Our house isn't far from here at all. The track curves out, you know, but if I go straight this way I'm home before I know it. You can even see our barn from the back porch if you know where to look. Bye, Josie," and she was off, running across the field.

Josie got home in plenty of time to put potatoes on to cook and slice a dish of cucumbers and onions. She was just sloshing on a little vinegar when Mama came in looking tired. She came over and put her arm around Josie.

"It's good to come home to a comfortable house and a healthy family," she said. "The poor young man I visited today is so sick, and he's all alone with only a dog for company."

"Will he be all right?" asked Josie.

"He might. I think he will," said Mama, as if she were trying to convince herself. "He has no livestock so he can stay in bed, and I told him I'd be back with more food. I'll tell Dr. Warren to visit him, too. But I had to leave him all alone. And there are so many like him." She went to take off her hat, and Pa came in just in time to slice some ham Mama had cooked earlier.

When supper was over Pa said, "Well, Christmas will come, flu or no flu. Isn't it time you children looked in the wish book?"

Matt's eyes lit up. "Tonight?" His voice was full of anticipation.

"Tonight it is," said Pa. "I'm going to town tomorrow and I'll take the order in."

"Same rules as last year?" asked Matt.

"The very same," said Pa. "Each of you put your names by five things you would dearly love to get for Christmas. And the chances are one or two of those things will arrive Christmas morning. There might be some surprises, too."

Josie got the Eaton's catalogue from the bookshelf and she and Matt began to pore over it. There were pages and pages of ladies with impossibly narrow feet and distant expressions. They were only useful for paper dolls. Josie turned those pages quickly, but she wondered whether women in Edmonton or Chicago really looked like that.

"I don't want to waste time on clothes, Josie," said Matt, so she quickly turned to the back of the thick catalogue where Matt's favorite pages, sporting goods and toys, were to be found. "All I really want is skates and a hockey stick," he said. "I want to get really good at hockey this winter. I think I'll ask just for those and maybe a set of Tinker Toys to build with. I don't want to waste my Christmas wishes."

Josie thought it was likely that Matt would get his skates. He had been using an old pair of Sam's and the clamps that held them to his boots had lost some of their grip so that the blades sometimes came off at crucial moments.

Once Matt had made his choices he went off to play Flinch with Pa. Josie was free to linger over the pages of girls' dresses. She picked out a beautiful corduroy dress in garnet red with an embroidered silk collar. It was a bit expensive but maybe she would be lucky. Just to be safe she also marked a middy dress. It was more practical and at least it came in bright copen blue. On the book page she chose *Beautiful Joe*, which was described as a charming story of a dog, and among the stationery and office supplies she found blank books, three hundred ruled pages bound in black with red leatherette back and corners. She should be able to write something wonderful in such a book.

For her last choice Josie turned to the page that showed "wholesome dainties at low cost." She would love to find some chocolates in her stocking.

Once she had made her own choices, Josie leafed through the catalogue looking for something for Mama and for Sam. She was knitting scarves for Pa and Matt but she was a slow knitter and two would be her limit. Besides, she had two dollars of birthday money to spend. She went back to the stationery page for Mama and found a box of letter paper and envelopes decorated with flowers. Sam's gift was perfect, a Boy Scout metal water bottle with a leather holder and strap for seventy-five cents. He was forever breaking glass bottles when he went for his exploring journeys on the prairie.

Josie closed the catalogue and left it on the table where Pa would see it. It was still November and Christmas seemed very far off. With no school to fill in the time it seemed even farther. Josie took *Eight Cousins* out of her book bag. She had better read it as slowly as she possibly could.

TEN

The Ferriers were just finishing their breakfast one morning when Mr. Graham came to the door. He was well over his illness, and neither Sam nor Mama had been by the Grahams' place for nearly a week. There were too many other people who needed help.

Mr. Graham didn't sit down. He stood by the stove, holding his hat in his hands. He looked thinner than before and there were deep lines in his face.

"Is Mrs. Graham well? And Margaret?" asked Mama, making her voice cheerful, though Josie could tell she felt something might be wrong.

"Yes, they're well." Mr. Graham stopped for a moment, then went on. "It's Dr. Warren. I've just heard that he has died."

"Died?" said Pa. "But I saw him two days ago. He said he was seeing patients from early morning till past dark so he was tired, of course, but he looked fine."

"I know," said Mr. Graham. "But apparently he came home at noon yesterday quite sick, and this morning he died."

"He was exhausted," said Mama. "I think the ones who push themselves and keep on working after they get sick, well . . . two of my bachelors kept right on going out to the barn sick as they were and they both died." She covered her eyes with her hands, but Josie could see tears running down her cheeks.

"He'll be sadly missed," said Pa. "He was a fine man and, God knows, we need a doctor now."

"There isn't another to be found," said Mr. Graham. "I did hear that a couple of nurses will be coming tomorrow. That should ease the burden on people like you." His glance took in the whole family.

"We'll keep on doing what we can." Mama brushed the tears from her face and sat up straight. "People are just so far apart and once they get sick they often can't even send for help."

"Don't you worry about getting the flu yourselves?" asked Mr. Graham.

"Of course we do," Mama said sharply. "I always wear a gauze mask when I go into a house. Whether that helps or not I don't know but it can't hurt. The children don't go into any sick person's house. They do outside things. And I've just decided we are not going to get exhausted. If any one of us feels even a little sick or extra tired, it's straight to bed. I hope everyone understands."

They all nodded, even Pa. Josie had not heard Mama speak so fiercely since the day they went with Angela to see Mr. Myers.

Mr. Graham put on his hat. "I'd better be getting home," he said. "My wife is doing some unpacking. When this terrible time is over I hope you'll all come for a proper visit."

Josie went to close the door behind him. "Tell

Margaret I said hello," she called after him, and he waved back.

For a moment the Ferriers were all silent, thinking of Dr. Warren and the two bachelors. Then Pa said, "Well, we'd better start our day. I'm going to the north. There are some families up that way I want to check on."

"I'm doing chores for Gregor's family," said Sam. "He's off working, and his father has been sick. He's better now but he's the kind who won't let work go undone, so I'd better get over there."

Sam and Pa put on boots and their warm jackets and hats. It was cold now but not yet bitter, and there was only a little snow on the ground.

When they were gone Mama said, "As for me, I have to bake and make a lot of soup. I'd better get busy."

"We could help, couldn't we?" said Josie.

"Oh, yes," said Mama. "You and Matt can certainly help." But she was such a whirlwind of measuring and chopping and mixing that both children kept getting in her way. Matt quietly left and went outside, and Josie finally gave up and went into her own room and sat on the bed.

Why did she feel so terrible? Surely she should be grateful that they were all healthy and could help other people. But that was it, of course. There was nothing useful she could do. She wasn't quick enough to be a real help to Mama or old enough to go with Sam and do chores.

"And anyway, I'm a girl," she said angrily to herself. "Even if I was fifteen they wouldn't let me ride off and do chores for people we hardly know."

As she sat there feeling more and more miserable, Josie suddenly heard Mama say sharply, "Oh, Lordy!" She jumped up and opened her door. There stood Mama with flour up to her elbows and her hands on her hips, staring into space.

"Mama, what's the matter?" asked Josie, feeling a little scared.

"It's the turkeys," said Mama.

"The turkeys?"

Mama went on as if she hadn't heard. "This is the day we have to kill the turkeys. Three ladies are coming this afternoon to help me dress them and we can't dress live turkeys. And I have to get this food ready for Sam and James to take out as soon as they get back."

Suddenly she looked at Josie. "You'll have to do it," she said. "Matt will help you."

"Do what?" asked Josie, though she knew the answer.

"Kill the turkeys, of course. They're not out in the yard so you'll have no trouble catching them. The hatchet is nice and sharp. I sharpened it myself, yesterday. Don't look so shocked. I know you want to help."

"Yes, I do," wailed Josie, "but there are twelve turkeys."

"Of course," said Mama. "That's why three ladies are coming to help. I'll give them two each and we'll have six to put in the grain bin to freeze."

"But how . . ."

Mama interrupted her. "You've seen me kill chickens. Well, this is the same. Wear one of my big gloves on your left hand and hold the turkey's head down on the chopping block. Matt will hold the feet. And then chop! That's all there is to it. We'll hang them on the clothesline to drain, and we'll be ready for the ladies this afternoon. Oh, and Josie, wear my old water-proof coat. There will be blood."

There was nothing Josie could say. She didn't like the turkeys but to personally chop their heads off . . . she'd never bargained on that. Ordinarily Sam would do it, or Pa. Or Mama would do it herself.

Matt had come in just in time to hear Mama's instructions. His eyes were round. "You can't, can you, Josie? Chop the heads off twelve turkeys?"

"Yes, I can," said Josie crossly, because she wasn't sure she really could do it. "But you'll have to help me catch them and, like Mama said, you'll have to hold their feet."

The first turkey did not make it easy. It flapped its strong wings and struggled to get away. Josie said, "I'm sorry, I'm sorry, I'm sorry," with her teeth clenched tightly together, while she forced herself to hold its head down firmly. She had to strike twice with the hatchet before she got through the neck. And there was blood.

Josie threw the turkey's head over the fence as far as she could and burst into tears.

"There are eleven more," said Matt helpfully. He looked a little green and blood-spattered himself.

"I know," sobbed Josie. "We're going to kill them all. It's food for us and the bachelors and everyone else. And turkeys wouldn't live through the winter anyway. But I hate it. I hate it but we're going to do it."

"Yes, sir!" said Matt, and Josie's sobs turned into slightly hysterical laughter.

Maybe the first turkey was the toughest, or maybe Josie and Matt got better as they went along, but there were soon twelve headless turkeys hanging by their feet from the clothesline.

Before they went into the house Josie shucked the bloody waterproof coat and helped Matt take off the old shirt of Pa's he was wearing over his jacket. Even so, Mama gasped when she saw them. "You've got blood up to your eyebrows," she said. "But you're all done? Good." She came around the table and hugged them. "That was a hard job," she said. "After you went out I thought, 'What have I done? Those are children!' But it needed to be done." She gave Josie an extra squeeze. "You've helped more than you know. Those turkeys will make a lot of soup."

"And Christmas dinner," said Matt. "By then I think I could eat turkey."

"Perhaps you would like something else to eat now. It's almost lunch time."

"I couldn't eat. Not yet," said Josie.

"Me, either," said Matt. "Maybe in fifteen minutes."

"I'd rather go for a ride," said Josie. "Could you spare us, Mama? I want to show Matt something."

"Wash your faces first so you don't scare anyone. I'll fix you some bread and cheese to take since you are bound to get hungry sooner or later. And you'd probably like a couple of apples, too."

Josie put on her warm jacket and wound her scarf around her neck. She still felt shaky. But she felt something else, too. Proud, maybe. She had done something hard that really had to be done.

She pulled her hat down over her ears. "Come on, Matt," she said. "Let's get some fresh air."

Ginger was glad to get out of the barn. Since school had closed and Josie and Matt had been sticking close to home, she had gotten little exercise. She trotted along quite briskly and rippled her skin with pleasure when Josie patted her neck.

"Where are we going?" asked Matt. "To see Margaret?"

"No," said Josie. "It's something about the silver house."

"I've seen it a million times," said Matt, who had probably never given the house more than a glance.

"Yes, but have you ever looked in the windows?" said Josie.

"Is there someone inside it?" said Matt in a pretend-scary voice. "A ghost?"

"No," said Josie. Maybe it had been a mistake to bring Matt, but she wanted to look in the windows again and not by herself. Matt was handy and he wouldn't be interested in the silver house for long.

The frozen grass crunched under their boots as they went up the hill. Matt ran on ahead. He went to the right-hand window, the one Josie called the parlor window in her own mind.

"Hey, Josie," he said. "Someone's living in the house. There's furniture."

"Yes," said Josie as she came up the steps. "But you can tell no one lives here. You would see their footprints in the dust."

"What dust?" said Matt. "There's no dust, Josie."

Josie looked in the window. It was easy to see into the room because the window was clean. How could it be clean? Josie blinked. Matt was right. There was no dust. The floor was clean and even a little shiny. The stove and chairs and table were there, but the dead flowers were gone. The vase stood empty.

Josie rushed over to the front door. The little panes of the square window sparkled. There was no dust on the stairs, and surely the banister had been polished. Matt pushed his way in front of her. He had to stand on tiptoe to look in the window.

"It looks nice," he said. "But who's living here?"

Josie didn't answer. She was looking in the other window. It was as grimy as it had been before. Inside, the dust on the floor was undisturbed.

"Look," she said to Matt. "That's what the whole house was like the day school let out. I promise. There was dust everywhere. And dead flowers in the vase. I don't understand it. Come on, let's look at the kitchen."

The kitchen was clean. There was no dust on the floor. The table was scrubbed and the dishes on the shelf had been washed and rearranged. The four plates and four saucers stood on their edges along the back of the shelf with the cups and bowls in front of them. The blue-and-white pattern looked cheerful in the pale sunlight.

"Do you think someone has moved in?" asked Matt.

Josie considered carefully. "There are no supplies. No cans of food or sacks of flour. And no hats on the hooks. No, I think someone has just been cleaning up."

Matt had his hand on the door handle. "It's locked," he said, and before Josie could reply, he ran around the house to try the front door. Josie was relieved when he came back saying, "Locked, too. Whoever it is has a key. Maybe it's Mr. McLeod. Maybe he's decided to move in."

"Maybe," said Josie, but she didn't want to think it. If Mr. McLeod moved in, the silver house would lose all its mystery. She changed the subject. "Let's sit on the front steps and eat our lunch. Then we can stop by Margaret's for a few minutes before we go home. I want to ask her something."

The cheese was hard with cold, and the icy apples made their teeth ache, but the food tasted delicious. Josie looked out across the land. "I love this house," she said. "I hope it stays empty so it can be partly mine."

"It's Mr. McLeod's," said Matt.

"I know, but he doesn't care about it and I do," said Josie. "So it's a little bit mine. Now I'll race you to Ginger," she added before he could argue with her. Matt loved to argue, but he loved to win a race even more.

When they knocked on the Grahams' door, Margaret came to open it. "I'm glad to see you," she said. "Are you all well?"

"We're fine," said Josie. "But we're feeling bad about Dr. Warren."

"I can hardly believe it," said Margaret. "He did so much for us. Oh, but please come in. Don't stand on the doorstep."

"Could you come out for a minute?" said Josie. "I

need to ask you something and we can't stay long."

Margaret said, "I'll be right back," and she was, with a coat around her shoulders. "What did you want to ask me?" she said curiously.

"Have you gone to the silver house lately?" asked Josie.

"No," said Margaret. "I've been busy helping my mother unpack. She still cries sometimes, but she says we need to be settled while we're here. Why?"

"I took Matt to show him what we saw in the house and, Margaret, someone has cleaned up the parlor and the kitchen. And polished the banister. I thought maybe it was you."

"Well, I wouldn't do that without you. Probably I wouldn't do it anyway. Keeping a soddy clean is enough work for me."

"I couldn't figure out how you could have gotten in," confessed Josie. "Both the doors are locked."

"And I can't walk through locked doors. You should have known that." Margaret looked in the direction of the silver house. "I guess I won't go there by myself any more. I don't want to meet this mysterious visitor unexpectedly." She smiled at Josie. "It's a pity, in a way. It was nice when it was just ours."

ELEVEN

"Being influenza-stayed is worse than being storm-stayed," Matt complained one gloomy afternoon.

Josie agreed. Even the worst storms blew themselves out in a week. This epidemic was going on and on. Pa and Sam were away most days, checking on isolated settlers and taking them food. Mama cooked and cooked. Then she went out in the buggy with big pots of soup and loaves of bread.

Josie and Matt helped as much as they could. Already they had dug two of the turkeys out of the grain bin where they were frozen hard as granite boulders. Mama used them to make turkey with noodles and turkey soup. Josie and Matt had become very fast at chopping onions and peeling potatoes. They were taking part in what the newspaper called "the heroic efforts of men, women and children to help those beyond the reach of medical care."

"Who would ever guess that chopping onions could be heroic," Josie grumbled to herself. She wanted to get out and do something, heroic or not. But she didn't say anything out loud. If she did, Pa would quote a long poem that ended, "They also serve who only stand and wait."

Josie privately doubted that the poet had stood

and waited. He had probably gone out and had plenty of adventures. She had finished *Eight Cousins* and was now reading Sam's book about King Arthur, so she was familiar with heroes and their adventures. She felt more like one of the kitchen maids in King Arthur's castle than a hero.

Mama, however, was much more than a kitchen maid. She went out into the world to help those in need. But today Sam came in just as she was getting ready to leave. He shouldn't have been home for hours. Josie immediately felt cold in the pit of her stomach. Who had died? But Sam just went over to the rocking chair and sat down heavily.

Mama looked at him for only a moment before she said, "Sam, you're sick." She felt his forehead and then took off her coat and hat. "I want Sam in a room by himself," she said to Josie. "Yours will be best. Go and take out the things you'll need for a few days. You can put clean sheets on Sam's bed for yourself."

Josie quickly gathered up some clothes and her school books. She stood for a minute in the middle of the little room staring at the new apple-green curtains and the shelf holding her music box as if they would never look the same again.

"Stop it," she said, almost out loud. "It's just for a few days." She took her things into the boys' room and dumped them on Sam's bed.

When Sam was settled in Josie's room, Mama sat down at the table with a cup of tea and talked to Josie and Matt. "We are going to take the very best care of Sam," she said. "He's aching and has a fever but he's not so sick. The important thing is for him to rest. I think it's safe for me to do my rounds today. Tomorrow I'll make another arrangement and stay home. Just make sure that your brother stays in bed. He's sleeping now and I've left water beside him. I don't want you to go in to him but you can talk to him from the door." She stood up and put on the coat she had dropped on the floor. "I'll be back as soon as I can." And she was gone.

Josie and Matt sat looking at each other. The room suddenly felt too quiet. They could hear the clock ticking and Sam breathing heavily.

Josie said, "I'm going to make us some cocoa and then we'll read to each other. Maybe Sam will hear, too. Have you finished reading the book Miss Barnett loaned you?"

Matt shook his head. He seemed afraid to speak, and Josie thought he was near tears. "We'll take really good care of Sam," she said. "Mama knows how. He'll be all right. I'm sure."

But she wasn't really sure and, of course, Matt knew that. There was nothing to do about it. Matt swallowed hard and got the milk jug from its shelf by the window where it was set to keep cool. When the cocoa was ready, Josie opened the book and began to read a story about a dog, but she could tell Matt wasn't really listening.

"I'll tell you what," she said. "At the bottom of every other page we'll go and look at Sam. Just to be sure he's still asleep. Okay?"

"Okay," said Matt, and he settled down in his chair. Each time they checked on Sam he was asleep, but restless. Josie read resolutely on, but the instant she heard the gate open and Lady stamping outside, she put the book down.

Mama came in with a gust of cold, fresh air. She set her empty soup pots on the stove and hugged both children. "I was lucky," she said. "I met Adam Martingale on my way and he agreed to do half the calls. He'll bring the pots back tonight and tomorrow he and his brother will do all the calls. I'll just make the soup. How is Sam? Has he woken up? I'll go and check on him."

When she came back she sat down in the rocking chair. "His fever is no worse," she reported. "That's a good sign. How about a cup of cocoa for me?"

Sam was sick for seven days. The third day was the worst. His fever was so high in the middle of the night that he didn't know where he was. Josie lay in her bed and heard him call again and again for Pa. Then he said in a voice filled with despair, "I can't see the house. I've gone too far."

"He's thinking of the time we were lost out on the prairie." Matt's voice came out of the darkness. "I was so little I didn't really know we were lost. Only Sam knew and he didn't tell me."

"I remember," said Josie. "Listen."

Now they heard Pa. "I'm here, Son. I'm here and Clara is here. You're safe at home." And Pa began to sing,

"Through pleasures and palaces
Though we may roam
Be it ever so humble
There's no place like home."

He sang on and on and Josie fell asleep.

In the morning Sam was better. He knew he was in Josie's room and he even ate a little of the soup Mama had on the stove. Mama and Pa looked very tired, but Mama said, "I think the worst is over. How do you two feel?" She looked at them critically.

"I'm fine," said Josie.

Matt said, "Me, too."

"No aches? No scratchy throats?"

They shook their heads. "So far, so good," said Mama. "Sam will be fine, I'm quite sure. Now I pray that the rest of us stay healthy." She drank the last of her tea. "Well, I have bread to make. You two go and give your father a hand."

They put on coats and boots and went out into a clear morning. It wasn't very cold, and they stood outside yawning and stretching. Pa came out of the barn.

"Sam seems to be out of danger so I'm going to see how some of the neighbors are faring. You two take care of the chores while I get ready. Matt, have a look at King. I think he's gone lame in his right front leg."

"Should I take him out of the barn?" asked Matt.

"Yes, let him out in the sunshine. But don't ride him. He just hasn't gotten enough exercise lately. We'll have to work him in gradually."

"I'll tell him Sam is getting well. I expect he's gone lame over worry for Sam."

"You might be right," said Pa. "I'm sure he's figured out that something is wrong."

"I'll look after Ginger," said Josie, and she went into the barn with Matt following. Ginger greeted her with a soft whicker and waited patiently while Josie filled her manger with hay.

Matt led King out of the barn. The horse was definitely favoring his right front leg.

They had arrived back at the house when Adam Martingale came in to pick up the food Mama had ready.

"I have a message for you all," he said. "I was at Pratt's yesterday and Mr. Pratt said to tell you that your Eaton's order has come in. He'll hold it until you can get in to pick it up."

"Our Eaton's order? Is it nearly Christmas?" said Josie. She really had forgotten that Christmas was coming. The influenza epidemic had pushed everything else aside, but Christmas would come anyway. Even without the school Christmas concert or decorations, it would come. At least there would be some presents.

"Three weeks to go," said Mama. "Plenty of time for the order to get here."

But one day after another passed. No one went to town. Mama wouldn't leave Sam. He was recovering, but slowly. And Pa was still making the rounds to check on neighbors.

Josie began to count the days. Christmas was coming closer and closer, and no one seemed to care but her. But she knew that when Christmas morning came, they would all think of those parcels lying unopened in Curlew.

Finally, during breakfast on December 19, Josie made up her mind. She stopped eating her oatmeal and said, "I could go get the Eaton's order." Everyone else stopped eating, too, and stared at her. "I certainly know the way and so does Ginger," Josie went on resolutely. "You let me go to town in the summer and right now the weather is fine."

Matt said, "I'll go, too."

"No," said Pa. "King is still lame. Josie will have to load everything on Ginger and if you go, there won't be room." He stopped, looking a little surprised.

"That means I can go, doesn't it," said Josie.

"Do you really think it's wise for Josie to go alone?" asked Mama.

"Well, everything she says is true," said Pa. "There are no signs of a storm coming up, and she's done the ride many times. She'll be back in time for noon dinner. You will have to use the saddle, Josie, or you'll have no way to carry the parcels."

"I don't mind that," said Josie. She jumped up before Pa and Mama changed their minds and quickly put on her warmest clothes—wool stockings and a heavy sweater. She went in to talk to Sam. He was sitting up in bed reading. He was very pale and he felt too wishy-washy to get up for more than a few minutes, but he was no longer sick.

"Did you hear? I'm going to go pick up the Eaton's order. We'll have Christmas after all."

"Lucky you," said Sam. "I'd like to be doing that job." He grinned at her. "I guess you'll do it just as well, though. But be careful. You know how the weather can change."

"I really do know," said Josie. "I've lived here just as long as you have, remember."

The ride to town was beautiful. There was hardly

any wind, and a thin dusting of new snow sparkled in the sun. Ginger seemed to enjoy the fresh air, too. She trotted along briskly and they arrived in town before ten o'clock.

"Good," thought Josie. "I'll be home in time for noon dinner."

She tied Ginger up and went into the store. For a moment she felt a little dazzled by all the shapes and colors and smells. It really had been a long time since she had been to town.

Mr. Pratt was minding the store alone. "Is Mrs. Pratt well?" Josie asked, and immediately wished she didn't have to hear the answer.

But Mr. Pratt said, "Oh, yes, she's fine. She's spending some time helping a family whose mother has died. This has been a terrible fall, but I hope and believe we're coming to the end of the troubles. I haven't heard of any new cases of flu for more than a week. How is your family?"

"Sam was awfully sick but he's on his way to being well," said Josie. "The rest of us are fine but Mama and Pa are busy like Mrs. Pratt, helping people. I've come to pick up the Eaton's order, Mr. Pratt. We want to have Christmas."

"I don't suppose you brought the buggy? No? We'll have to tie the bundles to your pony's saddle, then."

He came out from behind the counter with quite a heap of parcels. "There's one for the Grahams, too," he said. "From England. Could you take it to them? I'm sure they'd be very glad to get it."

"Of course," said Josie. "I've got plenty of time."

She and Mr. Pratt set to work tying the bundles all around the saddle until Ginger looked like a peddler's pony.

"I think there's still room for you. Give my greetings to your family," said Mr. Pratt, and he lifted Josie up into the saddle.

"Thank you," said Josie. "Have a merry Christmas." She waved to him as he disappeared into the store. Then she took hold of the reins and clicked her tongue. "Gee up, Ginger. We're going to see Margaret."

TWELVE

Ginger didn't move. She turned her head and rolled her eye at Josie.

Josie nudged the pony with her heels and said impatiently, "I know you're a bit loaded down, but the packages can't be heavier than Margaret, and you carry her every school day. Come on!" This time she dug her heels in, and Ginger began walking slowly toward the edge of town. Josie could feel parcels rubbing against her legs. It wasn't going to be a very comfortable trip.

Usually Ginger would begin to trot with little urging when she was headed for home, but today she was still plodding along with her head down when the last houses of town were almost out of sight.

"We're never going to get anywhere at this rate, Ginger," said Josie and leaned forward to give her a light slap on the neck. Ginger lifted her head and obediently began to trot. The bundles began to jiggle and then bounce. Josie shifted in the saddle, trying to settle the load.

A moment later she felt Ginger stiffen and step sideways, as if she was shying at something in the trail.

Josie said, "Whoa, girl. Did something startle you?" But there was nothing unusual to be seen.

The pony stopped, but Josie could feel her trembling. She sat for a few minutes talking to her quietly. She was getting very cold. She pulled her scarf up around her chin. They had to be getting on.

Once again she urged Ginger to a walk, and reluctantly the pony began to move along the trail. Her tail switched back and forth and she snorted nervously.

"What's scaring you, Ginger? There's nothing to be scared of." Josie made her voice as soothing as she could, but she was getting scared herself. They were moving too slowly. They wouldn't get home before dark at this rate.

She loosened her hold on the reins and clicked her tongue. Ginger began to trot. Josie felt a parcel bang against her leg, and the pony turned her head. Her eyes were wild. Josie felt her brain trying to understand what was happening, but it seemed to be paralyzed by the cold.

Then suddenly she knew. The bouncing parcels were spooking Ginger. Somehow she had to stop them from banging.

But before she could move or speak, Josie felt the pony's muscles bunch. Then Ginger was galloping. The parcels flew around wildly and Ginger tossed her head, whinnied, and raced faster. Josie grabbed the saddle horn and hung on as tightly as she could. She felt as if her breath had been left behind somewhere, but after a few long seconds, she managed to find her voice.

"Whoa!" she said, but she didn't shout. The only thing she could remember just then was someone telling her, "Never shout at a frightened horse." So she said in a voice she hoped was quiet and firm, "Calm down, girl. It's all right."

Josie said it over and over. Whether Ginger listened to her voice or simply got tired Josie didn't know, but she gradually slowed down. Finally she stopped and stood still with her skin twitching. Her breath made white clouds in the cold air.

Josie had a hard time making her hands let go of the saddle horn. At first she thought it was just because she was gripping so hard. Then she realized her hands were numb. In fact, she was cold all over. The sun was still shining, but the temperature must be dropping drastically. Maybe she should go back to town.

How far had they come? Josie looked around and was amazed to see that they had actually galloped past the silver house. It was too far to go back. The Grahams' place was closer, though now it seemed impossibly far away. How could she ever get there with Ginger panicking every time she went faster than a walk?

Josie thought of untying the bundles and leaving them by the trail, but her hands were so stiff with cold that she couldn't possibly untie the knots even if she dared to take her mitts off. If only she had a knife she might be able to cut the cords. Sam always had a knife in his pocket, but she didn't even own one.

She wished that someone would come riding along the track. But everyone else was somewhere safe and warm. All Josie could see was the patchy white snow stretching away forever and the silver house sitting cold and empty on its rise of ground. If only someone lived there. If only there was a fire in the stove and a pan of cocoa getting nice and hot. But there wasn't even any coal in that lonely house.

Josie closed her eyes. The silver house couldn't help her. She had to make a plan.

"We have to go on," she said to Ginger. "We have to get to the Grahams' house. But it's so far."

Then she remembered how the silver house could help after all, or at least its little hill could. "From the silver house I'll be able to see the Grahams' barn," she told Ginger. "Then Margaret's short cut will take much less time than the trail. That's what she said. We'll make it, even if we have to go the whole way at a walk."

Ginger did walk quietly to the top of the rise. Josie hoped desperately that she wouldn't have to dismount and go up on the porch. Surely she could see the barn from Ginger's back. She tried to remember exactly which direction Margaret had pointed. With great relief she made out the distant shape of the barn. But now she had another worry. Would the barn still be in sight when they got down on the flat ground? Whatever happened, they must not lose their way.

Josie shielded her eyes against the brightness of sun on snow and stared at the dark smudge of the barn. Pa had said something about this. Yes, he had said, "To be sure you keep going in one direction out on the flat land, line up two objects. Then when you reach the first, you go on to the second. That way you don't change course."

Josie looked for two objects that lay in a straight line between her and the barn. There was a clump of tall weeds—milkweed, she thought—with pods still hanging from the stalks. But what was beyond it? Nothing except a patch of ice, clear of snow. It showed up very clearly from the hill, shining in the sun. But would she be able to see it from the level ground? No matter, she had to get on. When she touched her nose she could hardly feel it. She managed to get her scarf up right to her eyes.

Going downhill, even at a walk, made the parcels shift forward and Ginger started to shy. "She can see them out of the corner of her eye," thought Josie. "That's one thing that scares her." She crouched down and managed to hold the parcels back till she reached the level ground.

Even then Josie didn't dare urge Ginger to go any faster. Instead she concentrated on keeping her moving steadily and calmly. The barn had disappeared from view, just as she had feared, but she could see the milkweed against the cold pale sky. When at last they got to the clump of weeds, she didn't have to find the patch of ice because she could see the barn, not very far off.

Josie nearly wept with relief, but now Ginger seemed to walk more and more slowly. It seemed to Josie they would be moving in slow motion toward the house and barn forever.

Then suddenly the gate was right in front of them. All Josie had to do now was climb down and raise the bar that kept the gate closed. Then she would be knocking at the door. Then she would be warm.

She opened her fingers and dropped the reins. That seemed to take enormous effort. She couldn't quite remember how to dismount properly, but she managed to get her feet out of the stirrups and then tip herself off the pony's back. She expected to land on her feet, but instead she fell over. Her legs wouldn't work. She couldn't bend them or feel them. They were numb.

Josie lay in the snow on her side looking up at Ginger. The pony lowered her head curiously. Josie could see that her nostrils were nearly clogged with crystals of ice. She had heard of that happening in extreme cold. That must be why her own legs were numb. Extreme cold, she thought dreamily.

She roused herself. She must not go on lying here. "Shout," she told herself. "That's the right thing to do." She lifted her head a little. "Help! Margaret! Mr. Graham! Help!" Her voice seemed to be swallowed up by the cold. Even Ginger only twitched her ears a little.

Josie tried to take a deep breath, but the air was so cold it hurt inside her chest. "Help!" she tried once more.

Ginger began to paw the snow, looking for a bite to eat, probably. Suddenly Josie was mad.

"You!" she said. "It's your fault. You should be doing something to save us." All at once Josie knew what she must do. It was risky, but it was the only thing that might work.

She raised her arm and hit the largest parcel hanging within reach as hard as she could. Ginger snorted and stiffened. Josie hit again. The parcel bounced off

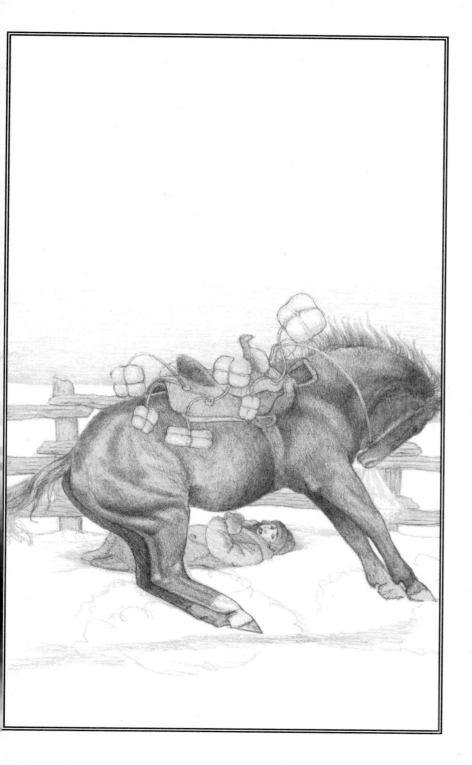

Ginger's side. Ginger gathered herself up and bucked. All the parcels began to bounce wildly, and Ginger bucked harder. She snorted and neighed, a high, screaming neigh. Just what Josie had hoped for.

But those pounding hoofs were dangerously close. Josie managed to roll herself right up against the fence. Thank goodness her arms worked. She didn't want to get trampled but she also didn't want Ginger to run, leaving her in the snow with no way to get the Grahams' attention.

Ginger didn't run. She bucked in a circle and neighed. Josie lay tight up against the fence, staring at the Grahams' door and praying.

After long minutes, just as Ginger seemed to run out of breath or fear, the door opened. Josie could see Mr. Graham. "It's a horse, all right," he called over his shoulder. "I can't see who's with it, but it seems to be loaded down with something." He stepped out onto the snow.

Then Josie called, "Mr. Graham, it's me, Josie."

He came swiftly to the gate and found her. "Josie, what happened? Were you thrown?" While he was talking he was catching Ginger's reins, calming her.

Josie said, "Please, I'm so cold," and couldn't go on.

Mr. Graham put Ginger inside the farmyard and then carried Josie into the house. There was Margaret, standing anxiously by the door, and Mrs. Graham, getting up from her rocking chair so that Josie could sit in it.

"Poor child," she said. "We'll get your things off." She unwound Josie's scarf, untied her hood and unbuttoned her coat. Margaret pulled off her boots.

"Her feet are like ice, Mother," she exclaimed.

"Get a pan of cold water," said Mrs. Graham. "We mustn't let them warm up too fast."

Josie felt as if all this was happening to someone else very far away. After what seemed to be a long time, she found herself sitting with her feet in a pan of cool water. She was covered with a dark red afghan and Mrs. Graham was spooning hot, sweet tea into her mouth, while Margaret rubbed her hands. Her feet hurt awfully but the rest of her felt quite comfortable.

"Oh, thank you," she said. "I have never been so cold. Is Ginger all right?"

"Yes," said Margaret. "Father unloaded her and put her in the barn. Whatever brought you out on such a cold day?"

"It wasn't so cold when I started out," said Josie. "It felt just ordinarily cold, you know."

"That's right," said Mrs. Graham. "John said this afternoon that he had never seen the thermometer drop so fast."

Mr. Graham came in just then, shutting the door very quickly behind him. "It's fifty below now," he said, "and it started at thirty, which is cold enough. Won't your family be worried about you?"

"Oh, yes, they will!" Josie was aghast. "I have to start home right now."

"No," said Mrs. Graham in a surprisingly firm voice, "you will not. John will go and tell your family you're safe and you will bide here till tomorrow."

"I'll go right away," said Mr. Graham, "but first

tell us what brought you to our door in such a condition so that I can tell your family exactly what happened."

"Of course," said Josie and tried to remember. "Oh. It's the parcels. The Christmas order from Eaton's. I went to get it and there was a parcel for you, from England. So I brought it along. Only the bundles spooked Ginger and I had to walk her and I didn't realize it had gotten so cold. When I got down to open the gate my legs were numb and I fell."

"But what made Ginger create such a commotion?" asked Margaret. "I've never heard her make such a noise."

"I did it," said Josie. "I banged a bundle against her and she got spooked. That's all."

"Well, your brain wasn't frozen," said Mr. Graham. "Thank God for that. You did well, lass. Now, I'd best be off before your dad comes looking for you. And I'll take your parcels with me. My horse won't mind."

"Don't forget to leave the one that's for you," said Josie.

Mrs. Graham looked at her eagerly. "You did say a parcel from England?"

Josie nodded. "It's all done up with red seals, so I think it must be a Christmas parcel."

"Then it will be from my sister Maggie. The one Margaret is named for. She's such a one for Christmas." For a moment she looked sad, but when Mr. Graham put the parcel in her hands she smiled and turned it over and over. Then she said, "I'll put it by till you come back, John," and laid it on the table.

After he was gone Margaret said, "Is there anything I could get for you, Josie? Are you hungry?"

"Not yet," said Josie. "All I want to do is doze off here by the fire."

"Then that's just what you should do," said Mrs. Graham. She rummaged in her workbox and brought out some mending. Margaret picked up *The Secret Garden* and began to read. Josie noticed, just before her eyes closed, that she was near the end.

"Good," she thought sleepily. "We can trade soon." It felt very restful to lean back in the rocking chair and let her mind drift. Her feet still hurt, but not so sharply. And she was warm.

Josie didn't wake up until Mr. Graham came in, bringing an icy blast of air with him.

"Getting a little rest, are you?" he said. "It's the best thing you can do. I met your father about halfway to your place. He'd come out looking for you and was very glad to hear you're safe and sound. I told him we'd keep you for the night and see you safely home tomorrow, weather permitting. He went off in a hurry to take the good news to your mother and your brothers."

"I'm glad they're not worried any more," said Josie, thinking about how anxiously they must have been waiting for Pa.

Mrs. Graham picked up the parcel. "I must open it now. I can't possibly wait till Christmas day," she said. She began to slide a pen knife under the red seals, taking care not to tear them.

Inside was a large tin, several smaller packages done up in brown paper and a dozen garlands made of intricately cut gold and silver paper. Josie exclaimed over them. One was angels with interlocking wings, another was girls in scalloped dresses holding hands and yet another had fantastic birds joined beak to beak and tail to tail.

"They're wonderful," she said. "We make snowflakes out of whatever paper we have. These are much better."

"It's my Aunt Maggie," said Margaret. "She makes them and she used to make me the most wonderful paper dolls, too. She taught me a little. I could try to show you."

"Oh, yes," said Josie.

Mr. Graham and Margaret strung the garlands from one wall to the other of the little house. They shimmered in the lamplight.

"It's festive," said Mrs. Graham. "Yes, it's festive." She thought for a moment. "We'll save the gifts for Christmas day," she decided, "but we'll open the tin now. Then we can have a bit now and a bit later."

"You know what's in it?" said Josie.

"I can guess," said Mrs. Graham. The tin was well tied up, but it only took her a moment to pry the lid off. Josie got a good whiff of something rich and tangy.

"My sister Amelia's Christmas cake," announced Mrs. Graham. She lifted out a square slab wrapped in oiled paper. Underneath the paper was a layer of muslin, and then, finally, a cake plainly iced with hard white icing.

Mrs. Graham set the cake on a plate. "There," she said. "Now we can have Christmas."

Margaret had been making tea during the unwrapping of the cake. Now she set out cups and saucers while Mrs. Graham took a long, sharp knife and began to slice the cake thinly. It was dark fruitcake covered by a layer of something Josie didn't recognize.

"It's marzipan," said Margaret. When Josie looked puzzled she explained, "It's made of ground almonds and sugar. We always put it on Christmas cake. It keeps the cake moist, Aunt Amelia says. Not everyone likes it. If you don't, don't worry. I'll eat yours."

Josie found she liked the marzipan better than the cake, which was packed with candied fruit and soaked in brandy. Margaret noticed how slowly Josie was eating her slice and said, "You probably want some bread and cheese. You must be starved." In a moment Josie was gratefully and greedily eating brown bread with good yellow cheese and apple butter she recognized as Mama's.

Mrs. Graham was enjoying the Christmas cake too much to pay any attention. "Amelia makes this cake in October and I suppose she thought it could age as well in the hold of a ship as in her pantry," she said.

She smiled, and for the first time Josie saw that her dark eyes could look happy. "The taste of it brings home to me," she went on. "That's Christmas, I guess. Thank you for bringing it to our house."

THIRTEEN

Pa drove the buggy over the next day to take Josie home.

"I know the Grahams would have done it," he told her. "I just want to enjoy your company." He hugged her extra hard, and Josie knew he had really come because he had been so worried about her. She was glad she would be sitting comfortably in the buggy with a blanket over her knees instead of riding Ginger. It was still very cold.

"I've never seen the temperature drop like that," Pa said to the Grahams. "We're used to bitter cold but that change was drastic. It scared the socks off me when I realized Josie had been gone too long. We're all very grateful that you folks were here and took such good care of her."

Mrs. Graham looked at Josie, who was painfully putting her boots on. Her feet were still tender. "Anyone would have done what we did, but I'm glad we could help Josie. We feel such strangers in this land. We didn't think we would ever begin to repay the help we've received."

She handed Pa a carefully wrapped piece of the Christmas cake. "This was in the package Josie brought us. I don't suppose you people have had time to prepare for Christmas and we'd like to share some of our Christmas with you. Josie will tell you about it. And, Josie, I'd like you to choose two of the garlands so you can decorate your house a bit."

"Are you sure?" said Josie. "I mean, I'd love it. Margaret, you choose. I could never make up my mind."

Margaret immediately went and took down the golden birds and a chain of intricate silver snowflake shapes. "The birds because I saw how much you loved them, and the snowflakes to remind you of this adventure," she said, folding up both of the garlands and giving them to Josie.

"Thank you for everything," said Pa. "Now I had better get this girl home, or Clara will get worried all over again."

They tied Ginger to the back of the buggy, and she trotted along as if she had never caused a problem in her life. Josie turned around in her seat to look at her. "Are you surprised that Ginger could get so spooked? She really ran, Pa. I had no idea she could go so fast."

"I wouldn't have predicted it any more than I predicted that drop in temperature. All horses have their quirks, though, and Ginger showed you one of hers. Tell me exactly what happened."

So Josie told him the whole story. She had to tell it again to the rest of the family when she was safely home.

"You were brave, Josie," said Matt when she had finished.

"I was scared," said Josie. "Very, very scared. But I couldn't just lie there in the snow."

"You kept thinking, that was the most important thing. And now you're here," said Mama. "I could hardly sleep last night even though I knew you were safe. I just wanted to see you. Now you're here and Sam is nearly well."

"And King is hardly lame at all," added Matt. "And we have the Christmas order."

"Blessings of all kinds," said Pa.

Christmas, when it came, was subdued but satisfying. The golden and silver garlands and some red candles Mama had been saving were the only decorations.

"And the fire in the stove," said Josie. "That's the best decoration of all."

Indeed, staying close to the fire and to each other was all the Ferriers wanted to do. Mama roasted two turkeys and put together Christmas dinners for Pa to deliver to three families who were still recovering from the flu. Otherwise they spent the day together, enjoying their gifts.

Josie was wearing her new Christmas dress. Not the garnet corduroy but one of blue and green plaid flannel with a pleated skirt. "It wasn't in the catalogue," said Mama. "I made it during the summer on Mrs. Pratt's sewing machine. I thought the colors would bring out the red in your hair." Josie felt completely satisfied. Pa had given her both the blank book and *Beautiful Joe*, which was nice and thick. Matt had spent all of his birthday money on a game of Parcheesi for the whole family.

Josie had wondered what Sam would do about Christmas. He liked to do last-minute shopping at Pratt's and at the lumber yard, but of course he couldn't do that this year. Not that he had to do anything. He was well. That's all anyone wanted.

But he surprised Josie by giving her his own knife. It was a pocket knife with three blades, all carefully sharpened. Josie knew it was one of his treasures. "I'll get another one when I need it," he told her, "but you need it now if you're going to go getting yourself into trouble."

Josie ignored his teasing. She felt the satisfying weight of the knife in the palm of her hand. "I'll take very good care of it," she promised, wishing, not for the first time, that girls' clothes had more pockets. Boys always had plenty of pockets.

Sam's present to Matt was even more surprising. It was a paper with a border of carefully drawn prairie lilies. In the middle Sam had written in his best script, "This document certifies that Matthew Ferrier is half-owner of the buffalo skull collection located on the Ferrier farm near Curlew, Alberta. The other half-owner is Samuel Ferrier."

When Matt read those words he was struck speechless. The skulls were Sam's treasure. He had found the first one the very first time he went exploring on the prairie when he and Pa were living in a tent and building the house. He had gradually collected eighteen, and they were arranged along the side of the barn where anyone coming to the farm could see them.

There were so many settlers in the district now that it was very hard to find buffalo skulls. Like the buffalo themselves, they were nearly gone.

Sam smiled a little at Matt's dumbfounded face. "You helped me find some of those skulls," he said. "They should be partly yours. Just don't go giving them away."

"I never would," said Matt indignantly. Then he laughed because they were all laughing.

After Christmas life settled down to almost normal. The severe cold spell ended. Most of the influenza-stricken families were back on their feet. Josie and Margaret exchanged books, and Josie sat by the fire and read about a big mysterious house in England.

Sam was hardly ever home, it seemed. In spite of the cold he went out for long rides, always with Gregor because Pa said, "Big as you are, Sam, something unexpected could happen to you just as it did to Josie." He was also helping Mr. Pratt add some storage space to the back of the store.

One day he came home from Curlew and said to Josie, who was reading as usual, "You're the one who got the good mail today." And he tossed her a long envelope.

She looked at the return address and exclaimed, "It's from the *Bulletin*! It must be an answer to the letter I wrote to Mr. Murray's friend."

"Well, open it," said Matt, who was busy at the table drawing pictures of dogs and horses inspired by the animal stories he had been reading.

Josie slipped the long blade of her knife under the envelope flap. "It's thick," she said. "I think he must have answered my questions." She took out the letter and read,

Dear Josephine,
Thank you for your most interesting letter. It's nice to hear from someone who is interested in facts and information, not just hot air.

The answers to most of your questions come from our file of U.S. newspapers. There may be some errors for, I must admit, not everything you read in the papers is 100% true. But here are some pretty good facts.

1. K.S. received her pilot's license six years ago in 1912. Her exact age is a mystery but probably she was about sixteen then, which makes her twenty-two now. She was the fourth woman in the United States to get a pilot's license.

2. She learned to fly at a school of aviation in Chicago.

3. She has flown in exhibitions all across the United States, and in Canada several times, mainly in Alberta (as you know) and Manitoba. She toured Japan and China showing off the wonders of flight. No other woman has done that and I suspect few men have either.

4. Besides all this flying K.S. helps her mother and sister run an aviation school in San Antonio, Texas, where she lives. Early in the war they trained Canadian and American pilots. She also drives racing cars in exhibitions. She volunteered for war duty as a pilot but was turned down because she is a woman, so she served as an ambulance driver in France.

5. She got famous by being a daring stunt flier and by setting records. She is, for example, the first official woman airmail pilot in the U.S. and Canada; the first pilot to fly with flares at night and also the first to use them to spell out words in the dark sky, and she is the inventor of the "dippy twist"—a loop-the-loop with an extra twist in it. She has set long-distance flying records and raised thousands of dollars for the Red Cross by flying from city to city to pick up donations.

I had the good fortune to hear Miss Stinson speak to the Press Club and I can honestly say that she speaks as well as she flies. She is a small young woman and attractive so I suppose it is not too surprising she is called the "flying schoolgirl" but she is clearly far more than that. She is capable and personable and very deserving of your admiration.

I wish you good luck in your writing project.
Yours truly,
Bill Stevens

Josie put down the letter. "Did he tell you what you need to know?" asked Sam.

"He gave me lots of information," said Josie. "I can write my report now. But I still don't understand why Katherine Stinson set out to do such amazing things. He keeps saying that she is the first woman or the only woman to do this thing and that thing. But why? What made her do it? That's what I want to know."

FOURTEEN

Josie was just thinking that January was going to last forever and that February would be even longer, when Pa came home with news. "The school board has decided to hold a winter term starting next week," he announced.

"Has the school board decided there won't be any blizzards this year?" asked Mama.

"Not quite," said Pa. "They've decided that blizzards aren't the danger they used to be. The wagon tracks are so well marked that it isn't easy to get lost in the snow." He looked at Josie. "Of course, we know this country can always throw something new at you. To be safe they're going to make sure that no child will be traveling to school alone. So, just for the winter, I want you three to ride together every day. John Graham will bring Margaret to meet you. I've already talked to him."

"Are you children ready for school to start?" asked Mama. "You had some lessons to work on, didn't you?"

Josie thought of all the spelling words she hadn't studied. "I know what I'll do," she said. "I'll write my report on Katherine Stinson. That will surprise Miss Barnett."

On Monday morning the report was in Josie's

school bag along with her books. It had very few blots and quite a few facts. Miss Barnett should like it.

Out on the track Ginger began to trot. The sharp *clop, clop* of her hoofs on the frozen ground made Josie brace herself suddenly and her heart began to race.

Sam looked over his shoulder and saw her sitting very straight, gripping the reins hard. He came to ride beside her. "This is the first time you've been riding since Ginger ran away with you, isn't it?" he said. "Don't worry. You'll relax. It's always like that after something goes wrong with a horse. Something in you is expecting it again."

"Has that happened to you?" Josie asked.

"Not with King." Sam patted his horse's neck. "But Gregor's big black horse, the one he called Chorney, he threw me once. He shied at a gopher and I went sailing. Gregor made me get right back on, but I sure didn't want to."

"I trusted Ginger completely," said Josie. "Now I don't. It feels strange."

"Well, you know her better now. Think of it that way. Something must have happened to make her so nervous of dangling bundles."

Josie looked down at Ginger's wide neck and ginger-brown hair. It had a curly twist to it that kept her from ever looking well groomed. She was a good pony. She just had a little twist, too.

"Well, she sure can buck. I never would have guessed it." Josie began to feel better. At least she had a really good story to tell, and maybe the other children would stop thinking Ginger was just a fat, stodgy pony.

Margaret and her father rode up to the fork in the trail just as the Ferriers got there. Margaret looked at Ginger a little apprehensively, but Josie said, "Don't worry. She hasn't changed. Sam says I just know her better now. But I don't think I'll ever ride her with a saddle again. And no bundles."

She gave a hand to Margaret so she could climb up, and they all rode on. As they neared the school they saw Miss Barnett standing outside with her coat and hat on, greeting the children as they arrived. Each group seemed to stop perfectly still for a moment before they went on into the building.

As they put Ginger and King into the stable, Sam said to Josie, "I'm afraid there's bad news."

Josie looked at him. Why hadn't she thought of that? Here was Sam alive and well, though skinnier than ever. It was hardly likely that everyone had been so lucky.

Sam was right. Miss Barnett greeted them warmly and then said, "I'm sad to tell you that little Phillip Larkin died of the influenza. His sister Hannah will be back at school in the spring but she is still too frail to go out in the cold. And the Greeley children won't be back. Both of their parents died and the children have been sent to relatives in Winnipeg. Everyone else will be back. And Sam, I especially want to welcome you. I heard you were very ill."

Some more children were arriving, and Sam was saved from having to say anything. Josie thought, "Five of us are gone." Phillip was a scamp of a boy who loved to run through a carefully set up marble game, scattering marbles in all directions. And the

Greeleys. Isabel was two classes down from Josie, the closest girl in age until Margaret arrived. She was the oldest of the four. Maybe that was why she was always so bossy. Now her little brother and sisters would really need her. Josie hoped the Winnipeg relatives liked children.

She was prevented from more thinking by the opening exercises. Miss Barnett had moved the desks so there were no empty seats, and she left no gaps in the day either. The children were glad to be back together from their scattered homesteads, and they worked with a will. At lunch time they played Fox and Geese and Red Rover, but Sam went into the school house halfway through the hour. When Josie went to look for him, he was sitting by the stove reading. "I have to do some extra studying if I'm going to keep up in school next year," he said.

Josie knew that he meant a school in Edmonton. She had no reason to be surprised but the thought made her feel sad. It seemed to her that Sam had changed. He went off by himself whenever he could. And he talked even less than usual. "He's thinking things out, the way he always does," thought Josie. "That's it. Only now he's making plans about his life. I guess he'll tell us when he's ready."

The winter term went on with only two interruptions for blizzards. Both started in the night so that no one had any doubts that the school would be closed, and both lasted just three days.

Toward the end of March, just when it seemed that the worst of winter must be over, Josie looked out her window one morning to see a perfect covering of snow smoothing all the roughness of the land. The ruts in the track, the stubble in the fields, the frozen mud around the watering trough had all disappeared beneath the even whiteness. This snow did not swirl and shift. It lay like a soft, cold blanket and did not move at all.

Josie dressed quickly in her room, not bothering to go to the warm space beside the stove. When she came into the kitchen Mama was setting bowls out on the table.

"I just want to go outside for a minute before breakfast," said Josie. "I've never seen snow like this."

"It's not real prairie snow," said Mama. "Or at least not Curlew snow. When we came out here I expected heaps of snow, but the wind usually doesn't let it lie long enough to get deep. Well, go on, take a look around. But don't go off without breakfast."

Josie put on her boots and coat and opened the door. She couldn't see the steps. They were buried in snow. She boldly jumped and landed up to her knees in a snowdrift. She could feel snow getting into her boots, but she didn't care. She turned around and around to look at everything. The house and the barn had bolsters of snow on their roofs. The pump, the fence posts, the grain bin were all decorated by plump cushions of white. It was all perfect except where Pa's footprints crossed the yard to the barn.

"It won't last," thought Josie. "I'm glad I was almost first out." She felt her way up the invisible steps and went in to breakfast.

The ride to school was beautiful, but it took a long time. The snow covered holes and ruts in the trail that were usually easy to avoid. Today the horses had to pick their way carefully so that they wouldn't stumble. Josie didn't mind. She was glad to have time to gaze at this new world without being asked to hurry up.

When they arrived at the silver house, even Sam and Matt stopped willingly to look. The house seemed to float on whiteness, held down only by the thick, soft layer of snow that lay upon its gabled roof.

"Silver trimmed with ermine," said Josie, very quietly so that only Margaret could hear her. "It really does look like a house from a fairy tale. And the windows are shining." Her voice grew louder. "All of them!"

It was true. All of the windows, downstairs and up, sparkled in the sun.

"But, Josie," said Matt, "it wasn't that way before. Remember?"

"I remember," said Josie. "Let's go look."

"We'll stop on our way home," said Sam. "We're already late for school."

Josie had to be content with that, though she could hardly bear to ride away. The day passed very slowly. Luckily the air was still and cold, so that even the sun had little effect on the smoothness of the snow. In the schoolyard, of course, snow forts, snowmen and snow angels made a new landscape. But the silver house, when they reached it, sat perfectly unchanged, as though it was under an enchantment.

"Let's walk all around the bottom of the hill before we ruin the snow," Josie suggested.

"Hill?" said Matt. "That's not a hill."

"It's the closest to a hill that we have," said Josie crossly. She was sorry that Pa's rules meant that Sam and Matt had to be there. They were not likely to appreciate this special moment.

Sure enough, the boys didn't walk slowly around the hill looking at the house from every angle. Instead they ran in a zig-zaggy fashion out into the fields and up again to the bottom of the hill. They were beginning to throw snowballs at each other when Margaret suddenly said, "Look! Footprints."

Josie looked, squinting her eyes against the brightness of the low sun on the snow. There were footprints, all right, leading straight up the back steps.

"Do you think the person is still there?" whispered Margaret.

"We have to go and look," said Josie. "Nothing will happen. There are too many of us."

"It might be Mr. McLeod," said Margaret. "He has a right to be here."

"But why should he come today? He's ignored the house all these years. I don't think he does have a right. Anyway, come on."

When they looked at the footprints more closely, they saw that they went down the hill as well as up.

"Thank goodness," said Margaret. "Whoever it is has pretty big feet but he's not here now. But where did he go?"

Both girls looked along the line of footprints. At the bottom of the hill they got all mixed up with the boys' footprints, and farther away the shadows and hollows in the snow made it impossible to tell what direction they finally took.

Josie knew it was unreasonable to be angry but she was, first at the maker of the footprints for daring to go up to and maybe even into the silver house, and second at Sam and Matt for heedlessly destroying the footprints. Without saying anything she began to stamp up the hill to the back steps. Margaret didn't say anything either.

"She doesn't want me to get mad at her," Josie thought. Suddenly she giggled, and Margaret began to laugh out loud.

"It seems so funny to be following footprints here," she finally said. "I feel like a detective."

"This person isn't very sneaky," said Josie. "If we were really detectives we could have tracked him to his lair easily. Instead we let the trail be destroyed before our very eyes. Oh, well, let's go see if anything has changed in the house."

They looked in the back window first. Nothing had changed. The dishes were still neatly arranged on the shelf and there were no marks of snowy boots on the floor. "I don't think the person went in," said Margaret. "No, wait. Look at this."

Under the window side by side on the dry porch were two snowy patches. "I think he left his boots here and climbed in the window. Shall we try to open it?"

"Let's not," said Josie. "Not until we can come alone. Let's just look in the front windows for now."

Margaret nodded.

They walked around the house and up onto the front porch, ruining the perfect pillows of snow that lay on the steps. Josie hardly thought about it. She went straight to the left-hand window. The glass was clean and shining. So was the room inside. Still empty, but clean. Margaret came and looked in, too.

"Somebody is gradually cleaning up the house," she said.

"And that's not all!" said Josie. She was at the parlor window. "Look at the table."

The vase on the little round table was not empty any more. Someone had filled it with dried grasses and milkweed pods, carefully arranged. They glowed faintly golden in the late afternoon light.

"That vase was empty last time, wasn't it? And before that it had dead flowers in it." Josie turned and looked at Margaret.

"Yes," said Margaret. "It looked so lonesome and neglected. Now someone is trying to make the whole house look beautiful."

"The mysterious visitor," said Josie. "But who is it? And why?"

Just then they heard the boys shouting. "Come on," called Matt. "We need to get home."

"Oh, yes," said Margaret, "and my father will be waiting."

The girls looked at each other. "Let's not tell anyone," said Josie. "Not till we know what's going on."

Margaret nodded. "I'll tell no one," she promised.

FIFTEEN

The soft snow didn't last long. It flattened and disappeared into the muddy ground by the time the winter term ended. Josie knew that spring had not come. April was a sneaky month. It let you shed your winter coat one day and dumped snow on you the next. Still, the worst of winter was surely over.

On the first day of the spring school break, she put on her jacket and went out to the barn to find Pa. He was busy checking harness.

"Time to get ready for plowing," he said. "What's on your mind, Josie?"

"I've finished my chores and I'd like to go over to Margaret's. I just want to have a visit and Matt isn't interested. And you know Sam, he's off somewhere. Look, Pa, the sun is shining and there's no ice in the puddles. Can't I go by myself? I'm sure there's not going to be a storm today."

"If I'm thinking about putting in crops I guess it's time to leave winter rules behind. But do watch the weather."

"I will," promised Josie, but she was not thinking about weather as she rode toward the Grahams' place. Her whole mind was filled with the silver house, swept and polished, just as she had always imagined.

Who could be doing it? She and Margaret had to make a plan so that they could find out.

But when she knocked on the soddy door it seemed that there was no one at home. Josie was just turning away when the door slowly opened. Mrs. Graham stood there, squinting a little in the bright sunlight.

"Oh, Josie, it's you," she said. "Margaret has gone to town with her father. Come in and wait for her. I don't suppose she'll be long."

Josie looked at her uneasily. She had no idea how to talk to Mrs. Graham, who was even more silent than Margaret used to be. But it would be very rude to just go away, and she really did want to see Margaret.

"Thank you," she said. "I'd like to stop in for a while."

She took off her boots at the door and looked around for a place to put her jacket. The house was looking much more lived in. The trunk was still in the corner with a wooden crate on top of it, but all the other boxes were gone. Now that her eyes were used to the dimness she saw that there was a row of hooks near the door, so she hung up her jacket and turned to find that Mrs. Graham was sitting in her rocking chair watching her. After a moment she seemed to remember that she should say something.

"Sit down, won't you?" It was as if she was saying a line from a play, a line she had almost forgotten. Josie sat down in one of the straight-backed chairs by the table. Mrs. Graham said nothing more.

Josie knew she couldn't keep quiet much longer

and she searched her mind for what Mama called a suitable topic for conversation.

"I'd love to go to England some day," she finally said. "Did you bring any pictures? It would be interesting to see some pictures of England."

Mrs. Graham shook her head slowly. "No," she said in a low voice. "We didn't bring any pictures."

"I don't suppose you had room. We couldn't bring much and we only came from Iowa. We had to bring all the tools and farm things, of course, so a lot of other things had to be left behind. We did bring a little furniture—a round table and the chairs that went with it and Mama's rocking chair."

"We couldn't bring any furniture," said Mrs. Graham flatly. "John had to build everything after we got here."

"He did?" Josie looked at the table beside her. It was made of narrow boards that were beautifully fitted together to make a pattern of squares. She had never seen a table like it. "He must be a master carpenter like my grandfather was. I think it's wonderful."

"Do you really?" Mrs. Graham sounded quite surprised.

"Well, we had to build furniture, too," said Josie, "but ours is nothing like this. Pa was so busy with the farming that Mama built most of it. She looked in the Eaton's catalogue and chose the kind of shelves and cabinets she wanted and then Pa cut the boards and she nailed them together. They're very useful but they're not beautiful like this."

Mrs. Graham didn't reply. She was looking at the table as if she hadn't really noticed it before. In the silence Josie began to think that she had not been fair to her parents so she said, "Of course, we do have some pretty things. Mama let us each choose one special thing to bring with us. Something precious to us that would remind us of home."

Now Mrs. Graham looked at her with a flicker of interest in her eyes. "What did you choose?" she asked.

Josie felt a little ashamed. Mama had never said the part about something to remind you of home. She had said, "Bring something that will help you feel at home in Alberta." That would sound like nonsense to Mrs. Graham, Josie was sure. Nothing would help her feel at home here in Alberta. But she could answer the question.

"I brought a music box my grandmother gave me. It was made in Switzerland and it's painted with flowers like a mountain meadow. At least, it's how I imagine a mountain meadow, beautiful green grass with little blue and white flowers sprinkled around. When you open it, it plays a waltz. It even has a secret compartment in the back, for treasures." She stopped. Why had she told Mrs. Graham about the secret compartment? Only Josie and her grandmother knew about it.

But Mrs. Graham surprised her. She looked her straight in the eye, and said, "Don't worry. I won't tell anyone. I know a secret when I hear one." After a minute she said, "Could I ask what your mother chose to bring? She did choose something, I suppose."

"She brought her rocking chair. She said it was a

large treasure but we could all share it, and we do. My grandfather made it out of black walnut from our farm. That's why I said he was a master carpenter."

Just then they heard the sound of the gate. Margaret and her father were back. Josie was glad, but she was surprised to find that she was not greatly relieved. It had not been so bad talking to Mrs. Graham.

The door opened and Margaret said, "Josie, I knew you were here. Ginger gave you away. Have you been waiting long?" She looked a little anxiously at her mother.

"We've been having a very nice visit," said Mrs. Graham. "Josie was telling me about some special things her family brought from Iowa, things to remind them of home."

Josie saw Margaret's face change as if a shadow had come over it. "She expects her mother to get sad again," she thought, and she said the first thing that came into her head, "You must have done that, too. I mean, you must have brought something because you loved it so much you knew it would make you happier to have it with you."

Margaret looked at her mother. "Yes, we did," she said. "Mother, tell Josie about the tea set."

Mrs. Graham looked toward the corner where the trunk and the crate sat. "The tea set," she said. "Not the blue and white dishes. Those are for every day. The Royal Crown Derby tea set. Service for eight. So beautiful. I got a cup and saucer when I married and I loved it so much that I added a piece whenever I could. My sisters gave me a cake plate for a going-away gift." Her voice was dreamy and her eyes seemed to be seeing something far away. Then her face tightened. "It hardly seems worthwhile to unpack it here. The table isn't big enough to set it out, and who's going to come to tea?" Mrs. Graham's eyes filled with tears. She reached out her hand to Josie. "Sometimes I worry that all the dishes are broken inside the crate. I'm afraid to open it to see."

"I'm sure they're not broken, Mother," said Margaret. "Don't you remember how carefully we packed them?"

"We could open the crate now," said Josie. "I'd get to see a Royal Crown Derby tea set and you wouldn't have to worry any more."

Margaret didn't wait for her mother to answer. She picked up a kitchen knife from beside the stove and started to pry off the top of the crate. She moved quickly, as if she had been waiting a long time to do this very thing. Mrs. Graham just watched her and Josie thought, "She's been waiting for this, too."

When the top was off, Josie could see that the box was divided into compartments filled with packages wrapped in soft paper.

"Did Mr. Graham make the crate?" she asked. Mrs. Graham nodded.

Margaret lifted one package out of its place and brought it over to the table. She carefully removed one layer of paper after another until she held in her hand a tea cup.

She turned it over and over, inspecting it carefully. "It's perfect," she said. "Not a chip or a crack." She balanced it carefully on the palm of her hand so that

Josie could see its graceful shape. It was white and deep blue and dark red and gold and it seemed to glow in the dimly lit soddy.

"It's lovely," said Josie. She had never seen anything so elegant.

Margaret held the cup out to her mother, who took hold of the delicate handle. She ran her fingers up the curved side and then pressed the smooth china to her cheek.

Margaret smiled. "So we have one whole cup, at least," she said.

"My mother would love to see it," said Josie. "The tea set, I mean. So would Miss Barnett and lots of other women. You could give a tea party!"

The minute the words were out of her mouth she was horrified. What was she saying? Mrs. Graham would barely talk to her, a twelve-year-old girl. She wouldn't want to invite strangers to her house. Mama alone would be enough.

But Mrs. Graham was looking quite interested. "Do you think some of the ladies would want to come to a tea party?"

"Why, yes," said Josie. "And not just because of the tea set," she added hastily. "They would like to get to know you."

"But the tea set would especially interest them, I'm sure." Mrs. Graham smiled as if she was making a small joke.

"Well, it is funny," Josie thought. "People can be awfully curious about their neighbors' lives." She smiled, too.

Mrs. Graham looked around her. "Of course,

there's nothing to be done about this house. It's dingy and small. How can I invite people to come here?"

"Everybody around Curlew knows about soddys," said Josie. "Lots of people have lived in them. They wouldn't mind at all."

"I'll think about it," said Mrs. Graham. "We have to unwrap the rest of the dishes and see how they are. I can't have a tea party if the tea pot is broken."

Josie almost said, "You could use another tea pot," but she didn't. To Mrs. Graham, the Royal Crown Derby tea set was the thing. Josie hoped that every piece was whole and unchipped.

Mr. Graham opened the door and came in. Fresh air filled the little room and sunshine fell across the table where Mrs. Graham sat holding the tea cup. For a moment he stood still, with the door open, looking at his wife.

She held out the cup to him. "Look, John. The girls persuaded me to unpack the tea set, and this cup, at least, is whole. Isn't that wonderful?"

"It is," said Mr. Graham. He started to go on but she interrupted. "They're even suggesting that I give a tea party. I could meet some neighbors and thank Mrs. Ferrier and Miss Barnett who have been so kind. What do you think?"

Mr. Graham seemed to be having a hard time finding words. Finally he said, "A tea party? Yes, a tea party is a fine idea."

Josie said, "We would help, wouldn't we, Margaret? We would help a lot." She stood up. "But right now I should go home. It must be getting close to dinner time and my parents will start worrying." Mr. Graham didn't seem to hear her. He shut the door and sat down near his wife.

Josie got her jacket and pulled on her boots. Margaret followed her out into the yard. "What did you do?" she said. "My mother has refused to open that crate ever since we got here. She said that her tea set did not belong in a sod house and that no one here would appreciate it. Now she wants to give a tea party."

"I don't know," said Josie. "I was just telling her about things we brought to Alberta because we loved them. Maybe she thought that other people out here wouldn't have brought keepsakes with them. Or maybe she's just feeling more at home now. I don't know. Do you think she really will give a tea party?"

"Yes," said Margaret. "I do. She sounded just the way she used to sound when she was hatching a plan. She used to be a great one for hatching plans. I just hope it turns out all right."

"It will be fine," Josie reassured her, but as she rode away she found herself thinking of all the things that could go wrong. "No," she said to Ginger. "If Mrs. Graham wants a tea party, she shall have it and it will be perfect. That is that."

It was not until she was halfway home that she remembered that she and Margaret still had to talk about the silver house. Well, now they had a perfect reason for getting together. The tea party would take a lot of planning. She would make sure of that.

SIXTEEN

As soon as she got home Josie told Mama about the tea party. "It's got to be a success," she said. "Mrs. Graham is so excited that it's scary. What if no one comes? Or she goes into one of her quiet moods?"

"People will come," said Mama. "That's not a problem. They want to get to know the Grahams and they certainly will be interested in the tea set. It sounds like a wonder of the world. As for Mrs. Graham's moods, we'll just have to take her as she is. If she doesn't talk, we will. You were very clever to think of a tea party, Josie. It's just the thing to make Mrs. Graham feel more at home here."

"Margaret and I don't really know much about tea parties," said Josie. "I hope you'll help us, Mama."

"I'll be glad to. Maybe you should have it in early May. The weather is more likely to be nice then, and people won't be overwhelmed by farm work yet. That gives you plenty of time to plan."

"I know we have to plan food," said Josie. "What else?"

"Well, who are you going to invite? And do the Grahams have chairs for people to sit on? And do you want to decorate a little to make the house look pretty?"

"I'll talk to Margaret about chairs and decorations, but who should we invite? The Grahams hardly know anyone except us and Miss Barnett."

"I'll think of two or three more people," said Mama. "That should be enough to fill up that little house."

"There shouldn't be more than eight altogether," said Josie. "That's how many tea cups Mrs. Graham has. So there's Mrs. Graham and you and Miss Barnett. We can only invite three more if you count me and Margaret for tea."

"It's your party," said Mama. "You should certainly drink from a Royal Crown Derby cup."

Josie felt better. Putting on a tea party didn't seem to be impossible and they had a whole month to get ready. And when she and Margaret got together they could plan about the silver house as well as the party.

Three days later she knocked on the Grahams' door again. This time Margaret answered. "Could you come out for a walk?" asked Josie. "It's almost like spring today."

"I'm sure I can," said Margaret. "Come in for a minute while I ask."

Josie stepped into the soddy. She stayed by the door because she didn't want her wet boots to turn the packed dirt floor to mud. Mrs. Graham was not sitting in her rocking chair but in a straight chair by the window, mending in a small patch of sunlight.

"Good morning, Josie," she said. "We unpacked the whole tea set and only one plate was cracked. John says he can mend it, so I suppose we can go ahead with the tea party."

"I told Mama about it and she thought it was a

wonderful idea. She says that early May would be a good time to have it."

"It seems a long way off," said Mrs. Graham wistfully, "but then I suppose there's a lot to do to get ready." She looked around vaguely.

"Don't worry," said Josie. "We'll get it all done."

"May I go for a walk with Josie?" Margaret asked. "I won't be long."

Mrs. Graham nodded and went back to her mending.

Without even speaking about it the girls headed straight for the silver house, tramping through the stubbly grass. "When spring really comes," Josie told Margaret, "the hill around the silver house is almost purple with crocuses. They are so small, but there are thousands and millions of them."

Margaret wasn't paying much attention. She was looking ahead at the house. "I think we should try that window to see if it's open," she said. "I want to know whether that's the way someone's getting in. Or is it someone with a key?"

"If it's the window it could be anyone," said Josie. "If it's someone with a key, it's almost sure to be Mr. McLeod."

"What kind of man is Mr. McLeod?" asked Margaret. "Do you know him?"

"Until this year he came and helped with our threshing," said Josie. "Then the threshing crew would go to his place next. He used to come in for noon dinner, eat as much meat and potatoes as anyone, only twice as fast, and then go out and check over the machinery while the rest of the men enjoyed their pie. Pa says that Mr. McLeod is interested in farming and nothing else."

"It sounds as if he doesn't have any feelings," said Margaret.

"I don't think he likes people much, but one time I asked Mr. Murray at the newspaper if he knew anything about the silver house. He said that he heard that Mr. McLeod would like to farm this rise of land, but he doesn't have the heart to knock the house down. So he does have some feelings."

When they arrived at the back steps Josie said, "Let's go around to the front first and see whether the mysterious visitor has done any more there." But the two front rooms and the hall had not changed.

"He must have come again," said Margaret, "or there would be at least a little dust."

They went up on the back porch and peered into the kitchen. At first everything looked as it had before but then Josie said, "What's that in the wood box?"

Margaret craned her neck. "It's some kind of paper and a few pieces of kindling," she said. "I'm sure there was nothing there before."

"So am I," said Josie. "Let's try the window. I hope it doesn't stick." But it slid up very easily.

"Just as if someone has greased it," said Margaret. She put her finger into the groove in the window frame and said, "See, I was right."

They both leaned through the window. "I think that paper is the Curlew *Star*," said Margaret. And before Josie could answer she had scrambled over the window sill and was standing in the kitchen.

For a moment Josie stared. It was strange to see a

real person standing where she had only imagined people before. Then she climbed through the window, too.

She pulled the newspaper out of the wood box. "It's last week's issue," she said. "That proves that the mysterious visitor was here very recently." Margaret didn't answer. She seemed to be listening. "Do you hear something?" asked Josie.

Margaret shook her head. "You listen, too," she said. The house was perfectly quiet. It didn't even creak. "I really do feel it's waiting for something," said Margaret, "but it's certainly empty now. Let's look around."

They walked the length of the kitchen, almost tiptoeing. It went right across the back of the house and felt quite homey with its stove and table and shelves. Margaret looked intently at the dishes lined up so neatly, but she didn't touch them. "Four of everything," she said. "Just the same as we have. I wonder if anybody has ever used them." She shook herself a little and turned away.

There were two doors that must lead into each of the two front rooms. Both were shut. Josie stood in front of one of the doors and said, "Let's look at the parlor first." It took some courage to turn the handle. What if there was something unexpected on the other side?

But there was the parlor, just as they had seen it so many times. It smelled faintly of wax and felt chilly, as if someone had let the fire go out. They looked at the two chairs of dark, polished wood and the table with its vase of dried grasses.

"It's strange that Mr. McLeod didn't have more

furniture," said Margaret. "Maybe his bride was going to bring some with her. I wonder what she would have put in this room."

Josie wondered, too. She knew the story said that the bride had never entered the house, but she kept feeling that she must have walked through the rooms before she took all her dreams back to Ontario.

"Maybe we're walking in her footsteps," Josie thought, but she didn't say it out loud. Instead she led the way back into the kitchen and around into the other front room. It felt very empty. Their steps echoed and their voices seemed to be too loud even though they almost whispered.

"Now the front hall," said Margaret bravely.

"Are we going to go upstairs?" asked Josie. The girls looked at each other.

"We have to," said Margaret. "We can't leave without seeing every room. It will be just like the downstairs. What are we scared of?"

Josie didn't want to think about that, so she kept talking as they opened the door to the front hall, looked quickly around and began to walk up the stairs.

"I always used to wish I could have one of the rooms with a dormer window," she said. "Especially when I didn't have a room of my own. I used to imagine sitting in that dormer window and reading. Maybe I'd even have a window seat where I could curl up."

Just at that moment they arrived at the top of the stairs and saw that the back dormer made a little alcove in the hallway just ahead of them. There was a door to the left and one to the right, both shut.

Josie went to the window and looked out. "Look, I can see your house!" she said.

Margaret came and stood beside her. "We really are close. Practically next-door neighbors." Then she turned toward the nearest door. "I can't wait," she said and opened it.

The room inside was L-shaped, with the short part of the L on the front of the house. There was nothing in the room but an iron bedstead in one corner. The floor was swept and polished.

"Look," said Josie. She was standing in front of the dormer window. "It's just the way I imagined. I could sit here and read and look up and see so far."

"Yes," said Margaret. "And you would put the bed right here so you could look out the window as soon as you woke up. And there's lots of room for shelves and even a desk. Of course it would be very cold in winter. But with piles of quilts it would be cozy." She sighed.

"Let's see what the other bedroom is like," said Josie. Out in the hall she paused for a moment with her hand on the doorknob. "I don't suppose there will be any surprises in here, either."

But when the door was just halfway open she froze. A still figure with long hair was standing by the window.

Josie couldn't make a sound, but her arm moved and slammed the door shut.

"What is it?" said Margaret.

"I don't know," said Josie. Her heart was pounding. "I thought I saw a person in there. But it can't be, can it?"

"I don't see how," said Margaret. "What did it look like?"

"It was a woman with long, wild hair," said Josie. "She was standing perfectly still. I could see her against the light, but I couldn't see her face."

"Well, I'm going to open the door," said Margaret. "You stay right at the top of the stairs. If it's anything terrible I'll scream and you run down and get out the window as fast as you can. I'll be right behind you."

Josie stood on the top step, ready to go down four steps at a time. She heard the doorknob turn but she couldn't see past Margaret into the room.

There was a moment of absolute silence. Then Margaret began to laugh.

Josie was really expecting to hear a scream so at first she couldn't understand what was happening. Then she realized Margaret was calmly walking into the room. Slowly Josie followed her. There was Margaret, over by the window.

"Look at your woman, Josie," she said, and turned around with a mop in her hand. "It was leaning against the wall with its mop head up," she said. "The long strings looked just like hair. For a split second I thought it was someone, too."

Josie felt a little foolish but mostly relieved. "Look," she said. "There's a broom, too, and some dust cloths. This is where the mysterious visitor keeps his cleaning supplies! Maybe he's just a very, very clean person who can't stand a dusty house." She began to giggle, and then both girls were laughing as hard as they could.

When they finally could be sensible again

Margaret said, "I keep thinking it's a man but of course it could be a woman."

"It could," said Josie. "But somehow I feel it's a man. I mean, my mama wouldn't just come in and clean an empty house. She would do something more. Maybe find a way to use it. Of course, this person may have more plans. There are some boards over here. I wonder whether they were always here or whether the mysterious visitor brought them?"

"Maybe he's planning to do some repairs, too," said Margaret.

Josie took one last look around. "I should be starting home," she said. It was getting toward dinner time but she also felt ready to be in a house filled with furniture and people. A house that was even a little crowded.

They carefully shut the doors to all the rooms and then the window, after they had climbed out. As they walked back to Margaret's place, Josie said, "How do you like the house, now that you've been inside?"

"I love it," said Margaret. "Now I can imagine living in it. I love all the windows and the wood floors."

"It's funny," said Josie. "I still like it, of course. But I think I loved it more when it was a house I could just dream about and furnish in my imagination." She fell silent, thinking that between mysterious visitors and scary mops, her lonely house was not so lonely any more.

SEVENTEEN

Josie was surprised by how quickly April passed. School started again and there was the tea party to plan. She and Margaret always seemed to be too busy to go into the silver house, but as they rode to school and home again they talked about the mysterious visitor and how they could discover his identity.

"There's no place for us to hide," said Josie. "No bushes or fences or anything. So we can't lie in wait and watch for him."

"And we can't hang around innocently pretending to do something because there's nothing to do near the house," said Margaret.

"Maybe we should just pin a note to the back door. You know, something like, 'To whom it may concern. We are two citizens who know that someone is going into this EMPTY house. Please leave us a note telling us who you are and why you are going into the house. If you fail to do this we will have to TAKE STEPS.'"

"Fine," said Margaret. "But what steps could we possibly take?"

"We could tell Mr. McLeod. It is his house. Maybe we should tell him anyway."

"But if he thinks the house will cause him trouble he might decide to knock it down and plow the land it sits on. I would hate to have the house gone. Or he might rent it to someone. That would be almost as awful. Let's not tell him."

Josie could feel Margaret's fingers digging into her waist. "You really do like the house, don't you," she said.

"Yes," said Margaret. "Even though I was a bit scared when we went in I felt right at home as soon as I was standing in the kitchen. I guess that's why I don't feel much like going in again. I don't want to get to loving it too much. Mr. McLeod could knock it down or sell it to someone any time."

"Whatever we do, then," said Josie, "we don't want to get Mr. McLeod thinking about the house. I guess we can't do anything right now."

So they went back to their old habit of admiring the house from the track as they went by. Their minds and time were taken up with getting ready for the tea party, anyway. First they helped Mrs. Graham spring-clean the soddy. In return Margaret came to the Ferriers' place and spent a day helping with the scrubbing and rug beating.

The difference made Josie appreciate the difficulty of housekeeping in a soddy. "You can sweep and sweep but you can't get the floor clean because it's made of dirt. And if you sweep too hard you raise clouds of dust," she told Sam as she rode into town with him in the wagon. He was buying some farm supplies and Josie was going to Pratt's to get special ingredients for the party refreshments.

Mama needed squares of chocolate and powdered sugar for a chocolate layer cake with fluffy white icing. She was also going to make little ham salad sandwiches spiced up with a touch of the bread and butter pickles. Mrs. Graham had listed brown sugar for a Prince of Wales cake and dried fruit for a fruit-cake. Without fruitcake it just wouldn't be a proper tea, it seemed. She also hoped that Pratt's would have lemons. Sometimes they did and sometimes they didn't.

Sam dropped Josie off at the store and went to do his own errands. When Mrs. Pratt saw Josie come in, she called out to her husband, "J.T., didn't a letter come in for Josie yesterday?"

"A letter for me?" said Josie. "Maybe it's from Grandma."

But when Mr. Pratt put the envelope in her hand, she knew it wasn't from her grandmother. It was a long envelope of an elegant creamy color. Josie turned it over and saw that it had a United States stamp. She read the return address: "Stinson Aviation, San Antonio, Texas."

"Oh, my goodness," said Josie. "It's from Katherine Stinson."

"Who?" said Mr. Pratt.

"You know," said Josie. "The woman aviator I was trying to find out about last summer. I wrote her a letter. I never thought she would answer."

Mrs. Pratt looked at Josie's excited face and said, "Did you come to do some shopping?"

"What?" said Josie. "Shopping? Oh, yes, I did."

"If you have a list why don't you give it to me?" said Mrs. Pratt. "I'll gather everything up while you read your letter."

"That would be wonderful," said Josie.

"You go and sit on that bench by the window. The light is good over there."

Josie sat down and carefully lifted the flap of the envelope. Inside there were three sheets of stationery, all covered with firm, angular handwriting in black ink, not hard to read at all. She turned to the last page. There was the signature, Katherine Stinson. Josie could hardly believe it. Katherine Stinson had written her a letter. It was amazing.

She looked at the signature for a long moment, then turned back to the first page and began to read.

Dear Josephine,

I am glad that you wrote to me. I often get letters from older people but not many from girls your age. I am pleased that I can inspire a young person like you even though you have never seen me fly.

I'm going to answer one question you politely didn't ask. How old am I? I'm twenty-eight now and I was just under twenty-one when I got my pilot's license. I was small with big eyes and the newspaper men decided I was sixteen. I suppose it made a good story. Once that age got in the papers everybody thought it was true. When I began flying in exhibitions I found that the reporters liked to write about me because they thought I was so young. I decided to let them think what they liked. Six years later they still call me the "flying schoolgirl."

I wanted to tell you the truth because you are young yourself. If you were to think that I was a successful aviator at sixteen, then you might think that you should be out doing something exciting in just three or four years.

Well, don't worry. You still have plenty of time to try different things and then change your mind. That's what I did.

All through my school years I thought I would be a concert pianist, but my family didn't have the money for the training I would need. I didn't know exactly what to do. Then by chance I got to go up in a balloon. I just loved it. Floating up into the sky and looking down on the earth thrilled me. In fact, the whole idea of flight fascinated me. I could already drive a car. Why not try flying an airplane?

I found out that it would cost $500 to take flying lessons—a terrible sum, you will agree. But I also heard that a skilled flier could make more than $500 for one exhibition flight. With just a few exhibitions I could pay for my lessons and also for my musical education!

I am grateful to my parents for helping me when I needed it. They sold their piano for part of the money and my father gave me the rest. Of course it turned out that I never needed a piano again.

I did have a hard time finding a flight instructor. Some told me I was too young (they didn't believe I was twenty) and too small, but I'm sure the truth is that they didn't want to teach a woman. When I heard that Max Lillie in Chicago would teach anyone truly interested in flying, I went to his school. Max made me proud by saying that I had a quick understanding of how an airplane works and a natural grasp of flying techniques.

After just four hours of instruction I flew the plane alone. Soon afterward I became the fourth woman in the United States to earn a pilot's license.

What I love most about flying is the freedom, and the fun. From an airplane you can see the pattern of the land. You can soar into the clouds or drop down to wave at a woman weeding her garden. You can fly in any direction. The whole sky belongs to you.

I am seldom afraid but once in a while there is real danger—maybe a strong wind or mechanical problem. It would be a little foolish not to worry when an engine fails and there's no place to land. But I have a lot of experience now and I have to solve the problem, so I can't waste time being afraid.

I have several ideas about the future. Right now I'm resting up. I drove an ambulance in France for a few months at the end of the war and came home exhausted.

I hope to be a pilot in the regular airmail service which is coming soon. This could be a fine profession for many women. I plan to do some exhibition flying but air shows probably won't be so common when airplanes are a part of everyday life. My biggest dream is to be one of the first pilots to fly across the Atlantic Ocean, but it will be a while before anyone can try that.

I hope I have answered all your questions. I wish you the best of luck. Whatever you decide to do in your life should be something you love. And remember, when you really want to do something, do not take no for an answer.

Sincerely yours,
Katherine Stinson

Josie finished reading the letter. She would have read it over again, but she could hear Mrs. Pratt thumping things down on the counter, and knew she had to tend to her shopping.

Josie told Sam about the letter as they drove out of Curlew. "Now I can understand how Katherine Stinson got started," she said. "She wasn't your age when she learned to fly. She was almost twenty-one. It makes much more sense."

"Do you know whether she had an idea of doing something special when she was younger?" asked Sam.

"She planned to be a concert pianist," said Josie.

"So she never was planning to be something ordinary. For a woman I guess ordinary would mean being a teacher or maybe a nurse."

"They're important jobs," said Josie.

"Well, yes, but it's like a man wanting to be a farmer or a storekeeper. It's fine but it's right under your nose. Maybe it's a good idea to at least think about doing something sort of unusual, even when you're my age or your age. You don't have to do it, but at least you can think about it."

Josie wanted to ask Sam about his plans. What was he thinking of doing? But there was the silver house, just ahead. Margaret was going to meet her there. They would carry the packages to her house and spend the rest of the day helping Mrs. Graham with her tea-party baking. She would have to ask him later.

Sam said, "Whoa, Goldie." He turned toward Josie. "I didn't think we'd get here so early," he said. "Do you mind waiting a bit for Margaret? I really need to get home. It looks like rain is coming, but you can wait up on the porch. I don't think it will last long."

"That's fine," said Josie. She was glad to be alone for a little while. She could read her letter again and really enjoy it.

Sam helped her carry the bundles to the porch. Then he ran back down the hill and drove away. Josie watched him out of sight. Then she sat down on the top step and opened the envelope.

EIGHTEEN

Josie finished reading the letter and folded it carefully. Without the envelope it would fit into the secret compartment of her music box. It was definitely a treasure. Something to keep forever.

She could put one of the newspaper pictures of Katherine Stinson in the compartment, too. Now she knew that it was a picture of a real twenty-eight-year-old woman, not a daredevil girl who seemed to belong in a story.

"Katherine Stinson is like Angela Barnett," Josie thought. "Angela has to find the right place to learn to be an astronomer just the way Katherine Stinson had to search until she found someone who would teach her to fly. And before they could search they both had to figure out what they wanted to do. And they had to ignore people who said, 'You're a woman. You can't do that.'"

She tried to imagine someone telling her that she couldn't do something because she was a girl. "I'm sorry, Josie," Miss Barnett might say, "I can't accept your offer to climb that ladder and hang the Christmas garlands. I realize that you have the ability to climb ladders and that you have hung more garlands than anyone else in the school. But the fact is that a girl just can't do this job the way it should be done."

Or someone might say, "I know that you want very much to learn the geography of South America but you just aren't tall enough and your hair is too long."

"That's why Katherine Stinson says that I mustn't take no for an answer when I really want to do something," Josie thought.

She was just beginning to consider what she might possibly want to do that would need such determination, when she realized that it was raining. How long had she been sitting here? She had no idea, but her skirt was getting wet, so she moved up onto the porch and sat with her back against the house. The rain fell harder and harder, pouring off the porch roof and splashing onto the parcels. Josie moved them back against the house, too.

She wondered whether Margaret had started off from home. Probably she was waiting until the rain let up.

The curtain of rain around the porch and the steady sound of it falling made Josie feel very far away from the rest of the world. She hugged her knees tightly and wished she was sitting inside a room with solid walls reading in the yellow lamp light with the rain pounding on the roof. That would be cozy. Here it was not cozy.

"If it wasn't raining so hard I could run around the house and climb in the window. Maybe it would feel better inside." But as soon as Josie thought of it she knew it wouldn't feel better. It was one thing to be in the house with Margaret for company and the sun shining through the windows. Even then it was creepy enough to make a mop scary. But alone, on a gray day, with the rain and the wind making the house creak... no, it was better to be out on the porch.

The rain was definitely letting up. Soon it would stop and Margaret would come.

Josie leaned her head back against the house and closed her eyes. "When I open them," she said to herself, "Margaret will be coming up the steps."

It seemed to her that a long time had passed, when she heard a muffled sound. She opened her eyes and looked for Margaret. There was nothing to be seen but dripping rain on wet grass. She hugged her knees tightly, held her breath and listened.

There it was again, coming from inside the house. It was a footstep. And another one.

Someone was walking through the empty rooms behind her.

Josie tried to think sensibly. Maybe it was Margaret. No, it wouldn't be. She would know that Josie would wait on the front porch. She would come and find her as soon as she reached the house. She wouldn't go inside and walk around. Anyway, this person sounded much bigger than Margaret. It was definitely someone wearing big boots.

The steps came closer. Josie was sitting between the parlor window and the front door. If the person looked out the window, he might not see Josie, but he would probably see the bundles. Then he would open the front door and find her sitting there.

The footsteps stopped, and Josie thought, "I can't just sit here. I have to be ready to run." She stood up and turned toward the front door.

A face was looking out at her through the diamond panes of the window.

Josie stared. It was a very strange face. A man's face, she quickly decided, but its eyes didn't match each other, and its mouth was crooked. It seemed to be a face with no expression.

Josie took two steps backward. She could feel her body wanting to run, but before she could move, there was the sound of a bolt sliding back. Then the door slowly opened.

The face became Mr. Graham's ordinary face, not smiling, but familiar. He stood in the doorway holding a hammer in one hand. Josie realized that she hadn't breathed for several minutes. She couldn't seem to speak.

Mr. Graham didn't speak either for a moment. Then he said, "I didn't mean to frighten you, Josie. What are you doing here?" He stopped and then touched his forehead with his empty hand. "I forgot that Margaret was coming here to meet you. I was in the barn when the rain started and I thought I'd better run over. There's a leak upstairs I've been meaning to patch."

Josie took a long breath. "You looked so strange through that fancy glass. It did scare me for a minute." She gave her head a shake to get her brain working again. "So it's you," she said. "The mysterious visitor is you."

"The mysterious visitor?" said Mr. Graham.

"Yes," said Josie. "Margaret and I like to come here and look in the windows sometimes. So we saw that someone was cleaning the house. We just called it the mysterious visitor because it was a mystery to us. We never guessed it was you."

Mr. Graham finally smiled. He stepped back out of the doorway and said, "Well, you had better come in now. You can sit in the kitchen while the mysterious visitor patches that leak and then we can talk."

Josie brought all the bundles in and put them in the kitchen while Mr. Graham went upstairs. The house didn't feel creepy any more. It felt like an empty house waiting for someone to move in. Mr. Graham was back soon, and he sat down opposite Josie at the kitchen table.

"I'm glad that you and Margaret like this house," he said. "I thought it was a good house as soon as I saw it. It seemed a real pity it wasn't being looked after properly. I worked on an estate in England, you know, and that's what I did. I looked after buildings. So when I saw this good house going to ruin, I couldn't keep my hands off it."

"We saw that you had swept and washed the windows and polished the banister. Did you do more than that?" asked Josie.

"Not very much," said Mr. Graham. "I just tightened up a few boards and rebuilt the back steps. They were pretty much rotted through."

Josie felt that she and Margaret had not been very good detectives. They should have noticed the repairs to the back steps. "I guess the mop and broom are yours?" she said.

"So you have been inside," said Mr. Graham. "Yes, they're mine. I put them upstairs to keep them out of sight just in case."

"We only went in once," said Josie. "We just wanted to look around but it felt so strange that we didn't do it again."

"Didn't you think the visitor was Mr. McLeod?" said Mr. Graham.

"I've been watching the silver house for a long time," said Josie. "I know that Mr. McLeod never looks at it. He only comes to work in the fields. I think he wants to forget about the house."

"The silver house," said Mr. Graham. "That's a good name for it. You know, in England we often name houses." For a moment his eyes seemed to be looking at something very far away.

"I still don't understand," Josie said after a minute. "I know it was very dusty in here, but dust doesn't hurt a house. It must have taken ages to clean it. So why did you do it?" She felt bold saying this to Mr. Graham, but she couldn't just go quietly home without knowing more.

Mr. Graham leaned back in his chair. He didn't look annoyed, just thoughtful. But before he could speak, they both heard someone coming up the front steps.

"That's Margaret," said Josie.

"We'd better let her in and tell her the whole story," said Mr. Graham. "At least you can be the one to open the door. That will save her a fright."

So Josie went and opened the front door. Margaret had been standing and looking toward the road, but she jumped and turned around.

"Josie," she said. "What are you doing? Why are you in the house?"

"Well," said Josie, "I've discovered the mysterious

visitor." As Margaret stared at her, she added, "There's nothing to be scared of. I think you will be very surprised when you see him. I certainly was."

She led the way into the kitchen and turned to watch Margaret's face when she saw her father. First she looked completely amazed. Then she started to laugh.

"Oh, Father," she finally said. "I should have known. You said it was a pity to see a good house go to ruin. Of course you had to try to save it."

"A house needs attention," said Mr. Graham. "Our English stone houses can stand more neglect before they start to fall down, but these wooden houses. . ." He shook his head.

Margaret sat down across from her father. "You hate living in the soddy, don't you?" she said. "There's not much fixing up to be done."

"I have to admit that a soddy is a very useful house," said Mr. Graham. "Ours kept us warm last winter. And it is good to use the materials around you when you build. But it's true. I love a house that can be worked on and improved. I've just been trying to decide whether it would be beyond the bounds of decency to carve a design on that plain newel post in the hall."

"Father carved the whole banister in our house in England," said Margaret. "And then we had to leave it behind."

"That didn't matter so much to me," said Mr. Graham. "I can always carve more. It's doing it that I love."

Josie looked around the table. It seemed so natural

for the three of them to be sitting in this kitchen, talking. "I wish you could come and live in this house," she said. "Would Mrs. Graham like it, do you think?"

Mr. Graham rubbed his hand along the edge of the tabletop before he answered, "I don't know whether the house would make a great difference. Her heart is in England and nothing here looks right to her. Anyway, Mr. McLeod won't hear of anyone else living on his land. That seems to be where his heart is."

Margaret ignored Mr. McLeod. "Father," she said, "if Mother is never going to be happy here, will we stay?"

"I don't know," said Mr. Graham. "I think there's a better future for us here and I'm coming to appreciate this flat land, but if it drives your mother to despair we'll have to leave. Of course we can't go back to England until the farm is built up enough to fetch a price that will pay our way back and some left over to get started again. It could take a long time." He fell silent and his shoulders slumped.

Margaret, too, was quiet for a time. Then she said, "I don't want to go back to England. It was so hard to get here and everything was so strange at first. But now I want to stay. I want Mother to want to stay."

"You're doing your best to help her," said Mr. Graham. "Both of you and Mrs. Ferrier, too. I just don't know whether she will be able to leave the old life behind. I guess some of us like new things better than others do. This is a new kind of house to me and I've enjoyed taking care of it."

"And here you could work without someone sitting sadly in a rocking chair," Josie thought. She noticed that the sun was back. It was shining through the window and filling the kitchen with warm light.

Mr. Graham pushed back his chair. "I think it's time for the mysterious visitor to gather up his tools and go home," he said.

"Will you come back?" asked Margaret.

"I don't know," said Mr. Graham. "Maybe I've done all I should do here."

"Maybe not," said Josie. "The silver house has been waiting for people like you. Maybe something will happen." It sounded right when she said it, but her mind immediately asked the question, "What could happen?" and Josie had no answer.

NINETEEN

J osie looked around the soddy and was satisfied. It
looked as beautiful as a soddy could look. She and
Margaret had covered the walls with white packing
paper Mrs. Pratt had given them. The rag rugs on the
floor were clean and bright. The small windows
gleamed.

All of this fresh cleanness had taken a great deal of
work, but Josie knew that no one would notice it.
The tea party guests would not look beyond the table
that had been spread for them. Mr. Graham had
made two new leaves for the table and it filled the
middle of the room. On it was arrayed the Royal
Crown Derby tea set. The elegant tea pot, with the
cream pitcher and sugar bowl beside it, was sur-
rounded by eight cups, each sitting properly on its
saucer. The rich colors glowed in the afternoon sun,
and Josie basked in the glow. It was a moment of
glory.

Besides the tea set, the table held three cakes—
Mama's rich chocolate layer cake with seven-minute
icing like drifts of snow, a golden-brown Prince of
Wales cake, and a neatly sliced fruitcake. "The best I
could do at such short notice," Mrs. Graham had said,
shaking her head. "A real fruitcake takes months."

There was also a plate of shortbread in fancy

shapes and another holding triangular sandwiches made of Mama's best white bread. Some were butter, some ham salad and some saskatoonberry jam. Mrs. Graham had been pleasantly surprised at the delicious taste of jam with such an outlandish name.

Everything was ready. Now Margaret and her mother were in the bedroom putting on their best summer dresses. Josie was wearing a green-and-white striped dress with a white collar. It was her absolute favorite at the moment because it made her feel like part of spring.

Josie straightened one tea cup on its saucer. She hoped that the guests didn't start to arrive before the hostess was dressed. Mama was on her way, of course, and Miss Barnett was bringing Angela who had come for a short holiday before starting the summer term at the university. That made six.

"Remember, we have to have eight," Josie had said to Mama. "We can't go to all this work and not use two of the tea cups."

Mama laughed. "That would be a pity, indeed," she said, "but it's certainly not a problem. I suggest we invite Mrs. Pratt. I think she would find the time and she is definitely a worthwhile woman to know."

"Yes, she is," said Josie, thinking of all the helpful advice Mrs. Pratt had given the Ferriers over the years.

"And, I think, Mrs. Leeman," Mama went on. "She's English, too, but she's lived here at least five years, so maybe she'd give Mrs. Graham a feeling that it can be done."

Not surprisingly, every person invited had accepted. Mrs. Pratt said, "J.T. will just have to do without me even if it is Saturday afternoon. You know the only time I've laid eyes on Mrs. Graham was the day they came in on the train and then she was across the street. A chance to meet her and see a Royal Crown Derby tea set? I wouldn't miss it."

Mrs. Leeman simply said, "Thank you very much. I'd love to come."

Now Mrs. Graham came slowly out of the bedroom. She was wearing a dove-gray, silky-looking dress with a high collar. Her hair was smoothly pulled back and her face was very pale. Her eyes moved nervously around the room and then settled on the table. She seemed to be counting the spoons that were lined up beside the cups.

"Are you quite sure everything is ready?" she asked Josie.

She had already asked this question several times, but Josie smiled encouragingly and said, "I'm sure it is, Mrs. Graham."

Margaret followed her mother into the room. Her dress was white with tucks across the front. The skirt and the sleeves were both just a little short. Margaret's cheeks were pink with either excitement or worry. Josie thought probably both.

Before Mrs. Graham could fuss any more, there was the sound of a buggy driving up and the gate opening. The first guests were arriving.

In no time the house was full of ladies, all wearing white dresses. Mrs. Graham greeted each one politely and then stood watching as they clustered around the table admiring the tea set and the refreshments.

"I haven't seen a proper tea set since I left England," said Mrs. Leeman. "And the very sight of shortbread reminds me of home."

"It's perfectly beautiful," said Miss Barnett, and Mrs. Graham's pale cheeks turned pink with pleasure.

"Please do sit down," she said. Then she sat down herself and watched Margaret and Josie pour cups of tea and hand around the cream and sugar. Josie could feel her eyes following every move. She felt like someone in a play, but it was a play without any words. No one was saying anything.

She looked desperately at Mama, who turned to Angela and said, "Tell us about university, Angela. How are your studies going?"

"I think they're going quite well," said Angela. "I've managed to convince the professors that I really do want to take mathematics and physics. They have decided that it must be because I want to be a high-school teacher. As long as I can move along in the subjects I need I don't really care what they think. I love living in the women's residence. I've met some wonderful girls and I've learned to play basketball. If I'm good enough next year I can be on the university team and go out to Vancouver for some games."

Basketball! Josie stopped with a plate of sandwiches in her hand. Now that was something she had never thought of. Imagine that playing a game could take you to Vancouver.

"You're very lucky," Mrs. Leeman was saying. "Before I married I wanted to study music. I had some gift for singing but my father said it was completely impractical unless I planned to give music lessons. My dream was to travel and perform, but of course he said that he wasn't wasting money on that."

"I am lucky," said Angela. "My parents simply believe in education, so they will help each one of us as much as they can."

The talk went on, but Josie didn't pay much attention. She wished Mrs. Graham would say something. She was sipping her tea and nibbling on a piece of shortbread. Margaret caught Josie's eye and nodded. Then Josie understood. Mrs. Graham was happy. Her tea party was going well.

Mrs. Pratt finished her first cup of tea and took a moment to look around the little house. "I always like to see how people go about making a soddy livable," she said. "You've made yours so pleasant." Mrs. Graham's lips tightened, and she set her cup down on the table.

"Perhaps it's time to brew more tea," she said to Margaret. But Mrs. Pratt would not be stopped.

"I'm always amazed at how resourceful people are about their houses out here where wood is so scarce. I've seen houses dug halfway into the earth. And there was a man who brought a whole freight car full of bricks from somewhere and built himself a regular Ontario farmhouse right here on the prairie. And when we wanted to add on to the back of our store we didn't bother to build. We just brought an empty house from the other side of town."

"The whole thing?" said Josie.

"The whole thing," said Mrs. Pratt. "Of course it

wasn't a very big house, and it fit perfectly onto the back of our lot."

"I mean, did you move it in one piece?" said Josie.

"Whyever do you want to know that?" said Mrs. Pratt, but she didn't wait for an answer. "They just put rollers under it and rolled it over, neat as you please. So you see, you just have to be clever."

"Margaret, would you light the lamp?" said Mrs. Graham. "It must be clouding over. The weather does change so quickly."

The lamp cast a warm glow over the table. Josie and Margaret cut the cakes. When Josie brought Angela a little piece of each, she noticed a spot of something dark on the white sleeve of her dress. "Probably jam," she thought. Then she saw another spot and another. They were appearing right before her eyes. She looked at Mama. Her dress was dotted with dark spots, too.

Josie looked up. She knew what was happening. It must have been raining for some time, and the roof was leaking. The sod roof. Mud was dripping on them all. She looked at Mrs. Graham, who surely hadn't noticed anything yet. What could be done?

Then she realized that something was being done. Everyone was ignoring the dripping mud. The women were talking and eating cake, paying no attention to the occasional drip that landed on them. She looked at Mrs. Graham again. Right in the middle of her plate was a drop of mud. She was staring at it.

Josie felt like crying. This beautiful party, so carefully planned, was ruined. "I'm like Margaret," she

thought to herself. "I want Mrs. Graham to want to stay. The tea party should have helped. Now she'll hate it here even more." She gave up passing cake and sat down to wait for something to happen. Something terrible.

Mrs. Graham put her hand to her mouth. "She's going to cry," thought Josie. "Everyone will feel awful and leave. And she'll feel even more out of place than before."

Then she saw that Mrs. Graham was not crying. She was laughing.

She seemed to stop a minute to catch her breath. Then she looked around the circle of women, all carefully balancing their Royal Crown Derby tea cups while mud fell on them. She laughed even more. And one by one the women joined in.

Josie didn't laugh. She could see Margaret watching her mother nervously. "She thinks that she's laughing because she's upset," she thought. "But it sounds like a real laugh to me."

Finally Mrs. Graham was quiet. She wiped her eyes with her napkin and said, "I'm sorry. I just suddenly thought of how ridiculous it is to play at being a lady when I live in a mud house. I never was a lady, you know. Just an ordinary woman with a fine tea set."

"It's what we all are," said Mama. "Ordinary women who brought whatever we could to this new place."

"You brought more than I did," said Mrs. Graham. "You knew how to cope. I don't know at all."

"You know how to put on a proper tea party," said Miss Barnett. "That's something."

"I didn't even do that," said Mrs. Graham. "Josie and Margaret did almost everything. And Mrs. Ferrier, of course. But I could have." She smiled. "I can serve tea on the prairie, for what good that is."

"If you can do that," said Mama, "you can do a great deal more. Look, it's stopped raining."

Now Margaret laughed and said, "At least we don't have to go outside to check. Shall I make more tea?"

"One more cup," said Miss Barnett. "I don't know when I've enjoyed an afternoon more."

Mrs. Graham smiled, a real smile of pleasure. "I may never come to love your landscape," she said. "I can't see any beauty in it, and the emptiness frightens me. But living here among you does seem possible now. I think I can do it for a while."

After the guests had left, Mama helped Josie and Margaret put the house back into its usual order. "I'll wash the dishes," said Mrs. Graham. "Then no one else has to worry about breaking them." But Josie could see that she loved handling each piece and carefully wrapping it so that it would be safe.

Margaret and Josie took the rugs outside to shake them.

"Mother is the way she used to be. All of a sudden. I don't understand it," said Margaret.

"It's not really sudden," said Josie. "She hasn't been so sad lately. Ever since she unpacked the tea set she's seemed happier to me."

"Today she laughed. It must mean she's happier," said Margaret. "But today was special. There were people with her. She'll still have to get through those long days when I'm at school and Father is working."

"But now she knows there are friendly people nearby," said Josie. "People who like her. Won't that help?"

"I'm sure it will," said Margaret. "It must."

On the way home Josie said to Mama, "Mr. Graham doesn't think that Mrs. Graham would be happier if they lived in a better house. What do you think?"

"When have you been talking to Mr. Graham about such things?" asked Mama, but she didn't wait for an answer. "If she really is willing to stay a while, I think a better house would make it easier for her to be happy. But a person can be unhappy anywhere, that's for sure." She looked at Josie and said curiously, "What's on your mind?"

"Just an idea that came to me this afternoon," said Josie. And then she was quiet for the rest of the way home.

TWENTY

The morning after the tea party, Josie went out to the barn while Sam was doing his chores. She took down the curry comb and began to smooth Ginger's rough coat.

Sam stopped cleaning out King's stall. "You have something on your mind, don't you?" he said.

"How can you tell?" said Josie, feeling unreasonably indignant. She didn't like having her mind read.

"You keep looking as if you're talking to someone," said Sam. "You can talk to me, you know."

"Well, you're right," said Josie. "I want to talk to you about an idea I have." She put down the curry comb and sat down on the edge of the feed bin.

"You know all about the silver house and how it's empty and how Mr. McLeod doesn't care a thing about it."

"Yes," said Sam. "Everybody knows."

Josie went on as if he hadn't spoken. "And the Grahams live on the very next section of land in a sod house. They need a real house where Mrs. Graham and all of them will feel more at home. Sam, Mr. Graham has been going in and cleaning up the silver house. He even fixed a hole in the roof the other day. He told me he used to look after houses when he worked on an estate in England. I've been thinking what a shame it is to have a good house going to waste so near them."

"It is too bad," said Sam. "But Mr. McLeod doesn't want other people living on his land. He'd never agree to rent out the house."

"I know," said Josie. "But now I have a solution to the whole problem. All we have to do is move the house off Mr. McLeod's land and onto the Grahams' place."

"You mean steal the house?" Sam shook his head in mock seriousness. "He'd be sure to notice."

"No, of course not," said Josie. "We'd explain to him that somebody else needs the house and he doesn't."

"I'm not sure Mr. McLeod would think much of that argument," said Sam. "I don't think he cares much about other people. Anyway, what gave you the idea of moving the house?"

"It was Mrs. Pratt," said Josie. "She said that they put a house on rollers and moved it across town to be their back storeroom. You know, the back room where you built shelves. So I thought of putting the silver house on rollers. It's not a very big house, really."

"I know it's done sometimes," said Sam. "When Pa and I built this house I realized a board house is really just a big box. Even big boxes can be moved. It would be a tricky job to move Mr. McLeod's house down the hill but I think it would be possible. That's not the problem. Mr. McLeod is the problem."

Josie thumped her knee with her fist. "I know that Mr. McLeod is the problem," she said. "But now that I have the idea in my head, I have to do something about it. That's what I came to ask you. What should I do?"

"A simple question," said Sam. "Give me a few years and I might have an answer."

"At least you've been around Mr. McLeod during the threshing. I've only served him mashed potatoes."

"Well, working with him doesn't mean you get to know him. He hardly ever talks. But Pa knows him a little. You should talk to Pa. If he thinks it's a good idea, he'll help you figure out what to do. There's one more problem I can see. Mr. McLeod might want quite a lot of money for that house. The lumber alone is worth a good bit, and he put weeks of work into it, too."

Sam went back to cleaning out the stalls, but Josie sat on the feed bin thinking until Ginger got her attention by stamping her feet and whickering. "Yes, Ginger," said Josie. "You want me to finish the job I started." And she did.

She didn't get a chance to talk to Pa until after the supper dishes were cleared away. He liked to take a walk around the farmyard in the evening, just checking on things. Josie hastily wiped off the table and went along with him.

She told him just what she had told Sam only this time she told it better. "Practice helps," she thought.

Pa listened right to the end without a comment. Then he said, "Josie, you've got a good idea. The part of it that would make the most sense to McLeod is that having the house gone would give him a clear section of land to farm. I know that he's determined to get the highest yield out of his land. He hates wasting even an acre. But that house does mean something to him, too, so there's no telling what he'll say when you put your proposition before him."

"What?" said Josie. "You think that I should talk to Mr. McLeod myself? I don't know if I could do it."

Pa looked at her thoughtfully. "Think about it," he said. "Is it a good enough plan to take to Mr. McLeod? If it is, then you're the one to take it. It's your idea."

"Would I go alone?" said Josie. She knew the boarding house where Mr. McLeod lived. Could she really go up to the door and ask for him?

Pa smiled at her. "I'll go with you," he said. "It's probably better if he knows you've talked it over with your parents."

"Thank you, Pa," said Josie. "I guess I have to do it."

Josie and Pa chose Sunday afternoon for their visit. "I believe that even Mr. McLeod takes Sunday off," said Pa. "We have a pretty good chance of catching him at home."

Josie remembered Mama's visit to Mr. Myers and was careful to look properly dressed and combed. She wore her second-best summer dress. It was plain blue and not so partyish as the green-and-white stripe. She asked Mama to braid her hair so that the curly bits wouldn't stick out. She wanted Mr. McLeod to take her seriously.

Pa drove the buggy, so Josie had nothing to do on the way to town but worry. What if Mr. McLeod wouldn't talk to her? What if he got angry? What if he decided to knock down the silver house so that no one would bother him about it again?

Pa must have felt Josie moving restlessly on the seat beside him. He looked over at her and said, "It's very possible that he'll say no, but if you don't ask him you'll always wonder whether he might have said yes. But I'm willing to turn around and go home if you say the word."

"No," said Josie quickly and firmly. "You're right. I have to ask."

"Good girl," said Pa. "I think you've got a good idea. Who knows? It might work."

When they passed the silver house, Josie saw it with new eyes. She had imagined it flying away to find other houses like itself. But what it truly needed was to be where it had people. If all went well it would roll down the hill and come to rest where it would not be empty any more.

Josie turned her eyes away from the house and toward town. She felt ready to talk to Mr. McLeod.

Mr. McLeod was at home, all right, sitting in the boarding house parlor, reading a stack of old newspapers. He stood up when Pa and Josie came in.

"Good day, Mr. Ferrier," he said. "If you're coming to ask me to work, I can tell you that I've plenty of my own to do."

"No," said Pa. "I know that you're farming a lot of land now. I wouldn't expect you to be available. My daughter Josie has a proposition to put before you."

Mr. McLeod looked at Josie as if he had never seen a twelve-year-old girl before, or at least never expected to have to speak to one. He didn't say anything. Josie looked at him for a minute. She had always thought of him as old but now she saw that he was no older than Adam Martingale. He had a narrow face and reddish-brown hair and very blue eyes with no hint of a smile in them.

Josie realized that he was waiting for her to say something. "I appreciate you listening to me," she said.

Mr. McLeod looked a bit impatient but he said, "Sit down. Please."

Pa and Mr. McLeod sat in easy chairs, but Josie chose a straight one. She wanted to sit up as tall as possible. "It's about the house that's out on your land," she said.

"It's not for sale," said Mr. McLeod abruptly. Then he seemed to realize that Josie was hardly likely to be offering to buy a house. "Well, go on."

"I ride by the house on my way to school," said Josie, "and I see that it's needing some repairs. Since it's empty it could get a hole in the roof, or the porch could start to rot and you might not notice. That would be a shame because it is a very nice house."

"I built it to be a good house," said Mr. McLeod.

Josie had to flatten her hands on her knees. They were sweating and she was afraid she was going to start twisting her fingers nervously. This was the hard part.

"I think it is a good house," she said. "A really good house. And my friends the Grahams live in a soddy on the next section. They really need a better house. And I know that you would like to be able to farm more land. So I wondered whether we could just move your house onto the Grahams' land and they could live in it. Then your section would be clear for farming and the house would be looked after properly." Josie stopped. She hoped she hadn't talked too fast.

"Whose house would it be?" asked Mr. McLeod.

Josie felt flustered. She hadn't expected this question and she didn't know the best answer. "I guess that would depend on you," she said.

"You're right," said Mr. McLeod. "It does depend on me. I built that house to live in but I chose not to live in it. It's still my house even if it falls down. So the answer is no, young lady. My house will stay where it is."

Josie knew that she should now stand up and politely say goodbye. But she didn't. "I know it's your house," she said. "But you don't love it. You don't put any care into it. It's as if you owned a wonderful piece of land but you didn't plow it and grow something on it. There are people who love your house. I do but I don't need a house. It's the Grahams who need one." Josie stopped for a moment to gather her thoughts. "Mr. Graham loves your house. He even fixed a leak in the roof because he thinks it's such a good house. But he won't do that any more. It's your house and we all know you can let it go to ruin if you want to. But I wish you loved it."

"How I feel about the house is not important. It's still my house," said Mr. McLeod. "I say no to your proposition." He stood up. So did Pa. Josie knew it was time to go.

Pa and Josie drove toward home in silence until they came to the silver house. It sat there as calm as ever, with its front steps waiting for visitors. Josie knew she would never go up those steps again.

"You spoke well," said Pa. "His mind is made up

195

for some reason we can't know. The Grahams will manage very well so don't fret."

Josie knew he was right. She guessed she was glad she had tried and she was very glad that she had said nothing to Margaret or her mother and father about her wonderful idea. At least they wouldn't be disappointed.

"Maybe when we're grown up I'll tell Margaret," thought Josie as she lay in bed that night. "We'll be living in the women's residence at the university and I'll tell her about the time I tried to get the silver house for her to live in. By then it won't seem so sad." The thought comforted her a little and she fell asleep.

The next morning she woke up with a dull feeling. "I guess it's because I hoped to be so excited," she said to Mama as she poked at her porridge. "I tried to be realistic, but deep down I had my heart set on telling Margaret that we would all help move the silver house right into their farmyard."

"It is a disappointment," said Mama, "but other things will come along to cheer you up." She stopped and listened. "I think someone just opened the gate. It's early for a visit."

Josie went to the door. She was astonished to see that the early visitor was Mr. McLeod. He left his horse standing and came up the steps.

"I can only stop a minute," he said. "I came to tell you I've changed my mind. It's a fair exchange if you people move the house off my land. After that I want nothing to do with it. I've looked at that house too long, I think." He looked straight at Josie. "In case you're wondering what made me change my mind, it was something you said. You said I wasn't putting anything into the house now. Well, I put a lot into it once and got nothing but sorrow. I'm better off with the land that is under it. Land always gives something back, sooner or later."

Josie started to speak, but Mr. McLeod went on. "It won't be your house but you say you love it, so I'm giving you a piece of it." Then he put his hand in his coat pocket. "I ordered this from back east when I was working on the house. I hoped it would give pleasure. Now maybe it will."

He handed Josie the brass doorknob from the front door of the silver house. He watched her surprised face for a minute and then said abruptly, "I'd like to put a crop in where that house stands, so I hope you'll be moving it soon." He nodded to Mama and was gone.

Josie stood there with the doorknob in her hand, tracing the pattern with her thumb. "He polished it, Mama. It was dull and now it shines." She held it up and it shone golden in the early morning light. "We can put it on our front door," said Josie. "After we have moved the silver house."

She put the doorknob in the middle of the round table. Suddenly the porridge looked delicious, and she could hardly wait to start for school.

TWENTY-ONE

"Whoa, Ginger," said Josie, and the pony stopped at the curve in the track where she was used to resting for a few minutes. She bent her head down and took a bite of grass. If she had looked up she would have seen that the hill ahead of her was empty. The silver house was gone.

It had rolled down the hill with the help of rollers, boards, ropes and a dozen people. Josie had watched it move slowly off the place where it had always been, lurching and swaying until it came to rest just outside the Grahams' farmyard. There it sat now, looking as if it had always been there. Only the porches were missing. They had been moved separately.

The Grahams had moved their furniture into the house, and their blue-striped dishes had joined the others on the kitchen shelf.

"Don't worry," Josie told Ginger. "We can go see it any time we want to. Mr. Graham will put the porches back on, and Margaret and Mrs. Graham are making curtains. Maybe they'll even paint it some-time. Then it won't be the silver house any more."

The thought made her a little sad, which was fool-ish since everything had turned out the way she'd wanted it to. Even Mrs. Graham liked the silver house. She was glad to come out of the dark of the soddy, as she put it, though she told Mama that now she couldn't hide from the prairie any more.

"I look out the kitchen window, and there it is," she said. "All that emptiness. It still makes me uneasy. But then sometimes I see Margaret coming home from school or you coming for a visit. This house is better, and I'm glad for it every day."

Josie was glad, too, but the silver house she had dreamed about for so long was gone. It had turned into something real. She would have to find something else to occupy her dreams.

The empty hill wasn't the only change. For the first time there was no summer session of the Curlew School. The winter term had been a success, and so now and forever more the students of Curlew district would have a summer holiday. The children liked it. It was better to be at home helping with the farm work in the summer than to be stuck in the house for endless bitter-cold days in the winter.

So Josie had a whole unoccupied summer before her as she rode to town for mail and groceries on this June day. She was glad to be off by herself to think about another change that was coming. Sam really was going to Edmonton when the summer was over. It wasn't a surprise. He needed to graduate from high school, and he could do that in Edmonton but not in Curlew.

Miss Barnett thought it would take Sam just one year to get his diploma. But he wouldn't come back then. He would go on to university. So it was true to say that he was leaving home. Now Josie would be the oldest, and Matt would be the only boy.

Everything would change. It made Josie feel very glum.

Mrs. Pratt didn't notice Josie's silent mood. She was full of chat about the moving of Mr. McLeod's house. "What an excellent solution to several problems!" she exclaimed. "Your pa told me it was your idea. Whatever made you think of it?"

"You did," said Josie, enjoying the look of surprise on Mrs. Pratt's face. "You told about moving the house from the other side of town to be your storeroom. It was at the tea party. Remember? That's what made me think of it."

Mrs. Pratt was truly pleased. "Imagine that," she said. "But I would never have thought of asking Mr. McLeod to give his house away. You get the credit for that. That took courage."

"It didn't feel like courage. I was very nervous," said Josie. "It just seemed to be something that should happen. I couldn't get it out of my mind."

"Maybe that's where courage comes from," said Mrs. Pratt and turned her attention to Mama's list. "Do you think your mother wants cheddar or farmer's cheese?" she asked.

Riding home, Josie thought that maybe Mrs. Pratt was right. Maybe courage came from wanting very badly to do something or thinking it was very important. Like Katherine Stinson. She didn't bother to be afraid because she wanted to do what she was doing. She thought about that instead of danger.

When Josie got home she put the groceries away and then sat down to read the Curlew *Star*. When she turned to the inside page a large advertisement caught her eye.

COME TO THE FAIR AT SCANDA
GRAND FINALE SATURDAY
AIR SHOW STARRING
CAPTAIN JERRY MULDOON
OF THE R.A.F.
SEE AMAZING FEATS OF FLYING!

At dinner Josie said, "Pa, you told me once that I might be able to see an air show at the fair at Scanda sometime. Well, it's happening next week. Could we go?" And she handed him the newspaper.

Matt craned his neck to see the advertisement. "Why do you want to go, Josie? I thought Katherine Stinson was the aviator you wanted to see."

"Well, of course I want to see Katherine Stinson most of all," said Josie. "But I've never even seen an airplane, let alone an exhibition of flying."

"And we could see the rest of the fair, too," said Matt.

"How about you, Sam?" said Pa. "Do you want to see the air show?"

"Not as much as Josie does. But sure, I'd like to go."

"I'm too busy to go myself," said Pa. "What about you, Clara?"

"That day I have a Farm Women's meeting. It's the first of the summer and I don't want to miss it," said Mama. "But you three can go. You'll have a good time on your own."

And so it happened that Josie, Matt and Sam started off in the buggy very early Saturday morning. It would take about two and a half hours to get to

Scanda, Pa reckoned. The air show started at 1:00 so they would be there in plenty of time.

Matt and Sam both wanted to look around the fair. There would be exhibits of farm produce and animals and a midway with rides and games. Josie could think of nothing but the air show.

"Do you think that Jerry Muldoon might know Katherine Stinson?" she asked Sam.

"I'd be surprised if he did," said Sam. "He was over in Europe flying with the R.A.F. He wouldn't have been going around to exhibitions in the last few years. But you might be able to ask him. I think the performers will be around to talk to the crowd. Scanda isn't that big."

But when the Ferriers arrived at the fairgrounds, it seemed to Josie that everybody in Alberta except for Pa and Mama must be there. There were rows of buggies and wagons and horses and quite a few automobiles, too. Scanda was a bigger center than Curlew and proudly proclaimed five miles of graded road in all directions.

Sam got the horses settled and then said to Matt and Josie, "If you get lost, go and stand by the Ferris wheel. You can see it from anywhere. But let's try to stick together. It will save a lot of trouble." Then they plunged into the world of the fair.

They went first to look at the animal judging and admired the biggest pigs, the cleanest cows and the highest-stepping horses they had ever seen. Then they all got hungry looking at tables of prize-winning baked goods and preserves. By then it was eleven-thirty.

"We'll go to the food tent," said Sam. "Then we'll

have time to walk along the midway before the air show."

But after they had eaten chicken pot pie followed by lemon cake, all prepared by the Presbyterian Women, Josie said, "I don't want to look at the midway. I'll go and find a place in the grandstand. I'll save you seats."

"All right," said Sam. "Sit by an aisle near the front so we'll be able to find you."

When Josie got to the grandstand, it was nearly empty. The horse racing was over and most people had gone off to eat lunch. She chose three seats in the fourth row and marked them with her jacket and hat.

She noticed four men standing at the edge of the field, talking intently. After a few minutes, three of them hurried away. The remaining man was tall and thin. He wore a leather coat and high boots. Something dangled from his hand. After a minute Josie realized it was a leather helmet. The kind fliers wore.

"That must be Jerry Muldoon," she said to herself. He was pacing up and down as if he was waiting for something. "I could talk to him now, while hardly anyone is around."

Josie climbed down to the bottom of the grandstand. Jerry Muldoon was still pacing, and he didn't notice her until she was standing right beside him. Then he smiled and stuck out his hand.

"Hello," he said. "Have you come to see my show?"

"Yes," said Josie. She stuck out her hand, too, so that he could shake it. "My brothers and I drove over from Curlew this morning just to see you fly."

"I don't think I've ever heard of Curlew," said Jerry Muldoon.

"I'm not surprised," said Josie. "It's not very near and it's just a little town. We don't even live there. We live on a farm."

"And you came all this way to see an air show?" Jerry Muldoon raised his eyebrows.

"I had a special reason," said Josie. "I got interested in Katherine Stinson last year when she flew the air mail from Calgary to Edmonton. I read all about her in the newspaper and I thought she was wonderful. But I've never seen a real airplane or an aviator. So when I saw the notice about your show I thought, this is my chance."

"Katherine Stinson, eh," said Jerry Muldoon. "I saw her fly once. It was in New York state somewhere at the very beginning of the war. My father was a nut about airplanes, and he used to take me to see any show we could get to from southern Ontario. Of course in those days I never thought I'd be putting on a show myself one day."

"You really saw Katherine Stinson? What was she like?"

"Well, I was only a kid then, remember. She was a little thing but she walked very straight and checked everything over before she went up. She's never had an accident, you know. But she's a daring flier. She did some fancy loops, like nothing I'd ever seen before."

"Do you know what she's doing now? Will she ever come to Canada again, do you think?"

"She'll probably have a hard time getting booked into exhibitions now. You see, we're all back. The men who flew during the war. I think the women will have to step aside. We can put on the air shows now."

"But she wanted to fly during the war!" said Josie. "She tried to get into the air force but they wouldn't take her because she's a woman."

"Well, they couldn't, could they? I mean, women don't take part in wars."

"She did take part. She drove an ambulance since they wouldn't let her fly."

"She's got courage," said Jerry Muldoon. "I'll give her that. But I don't think she'll get back on the circuit. I hear her health isn't good right now anyway."

"I think that's because of driving the ambulance," said Josie. "But she won't give up. I know she won't."

Jerry Muldoon grinned. "It sounds to me as if the two of you are cut out of the same piece of cloth. I wonder what plans you have for your life."

Before Josie could think of a reply, there was a shout from the end of the field.

"They've brought my airplane out," said Jerry Muldoon. "I have to get on with my job. I hope you enjoy my show." He gave her hand another shake and went off, putting on his helmet.

Josie could see the airplane at the end of the field. It looked small and flimsy but Mr. Muldoon strode toward it confidently. He seemed to have no doubt about his future.

She found Matt and Sam waiting for her in the grandstand, which was rapidly filling up with excited people.

"That was Jerry Muldoon, wasn't it?" said Matt. "Did you like him? Did he tell you anything interesting?"

"I did like him," said Josie. "But I have to think about what he told me. It was interesting but I didn't like it much."

There was no time to explain because Jerry Muldoon had climbed into the cockpit. A mechanic whirled the propeller. The engine's sputtering smoothed out into a thin roar. The plane rolled along the field in front of the grandstand, going faster and faster. Josie could see Jerry Muldoon inside, looking straight ahead. Then the plane was off the ground. Josie drew in her breath as if she would rise with it. Of course, she had known what would happen, but to see that machine with a large man in it soar up into the sky was truly amazing.

Jerry Muldoon did all the tricks Josie had read about. He did loop-the-loops and flew upside down. He took the airplane up so high that it was just a dot against the blue sky. Then he brought it down in a spiral that made her dizzy. He flew over the crowd and dropped a flurry of colored paper squares with "The High-flying Jerry Muldoon" printed on them. Josie caught a blue one right out of the air. Sam and Matt gathered up enough from the ground to take to all their friends.

When at last Jerry Muldoon landed, Josie wanted to forgive him for his wrong-headed ideas about Katherine Stinson. But she couldn't.

"Do you think Katherine Stinson or any other woman should give up flying so that the men who were pilots in the war can put on the exhibitions?" she asked Sam and Matt as they drove home.

"Is that what Jerry Muldoon said?" Sam asked.

"That's what he said. I know it's because he wants to keep flying himself, but it's not fair."

"I guess that men like him had a hard time of it. Now they just want to work."

"But that's not Katherine Stinson's fault and she wants to work, too," said Josie. "I wonder what she would say to Jerry Muldoon."

For a while they rode along in silence. They were not far from home now but Josie seldom came in this direction. The track here went along a kind of gully where a stream would flow after a heavy rain. On the other side of the gully was unplowed prairie.

Sam said, "I come out here sometimes. I like to see the prairie the way it was when we came. And I found something right here that gave me an idea. I'll show it to you."

He drove the buggy off the track and left the horses to stand while he led Josie and Matt across the gully and up onto the springy grass of the prairie. He walked slowly, studying the ground. Suddenly he stopped.

"Look," he said. Josie and Matt both looked at the ground. Sam waited. "Don't you see anything?" he finally asked.

"Yes," said Josie. "I do. I see a circle cut into the earth. We're standing in the middle of it. What is it, Sam?"

"It's a tepee ring," said Sam. "The Indians who lived here before the settlers arrived used to come this way to hunt buffalo, and they always camped in the same spot. Every year they put a tepee right here and they did it for so many years that they wore a circle in the earth. There are more nearby. I've counted eight."

"It's wonderful," said Josie. "But what do tepee rings have to do with you?"

"I want to know more," said Sam. "I've only been here three years and I've seen so much land plowed for the first time. I've plowed some of it up myself. I used to be able to find buffalo skulls, but I think they're all gone now. I've wondered about the buffalo ever since I found that first skull. Now I wonder about all the animals and people that were here before. I hope I can study about it in university."

Josie traced the circle of the tepee ring with her eyes. It had been here so long. Even when the people who had made it were gone, the circle remained.

Sam was watching her. "This is a good place to come and sit when you want to think," he said. "I'd be glad if you'd come here sometimes."

"I will," said Josie. "Maybe I'll come here and figure out what I'm going to do in the world. Maybe I'll bring Margaret some day. She'd like it, too."

"Good," said Sam. "That's my going-away present to you. And as for you," he said to Matt. "I'm going to give you King. You'll have to share him with me when I'm at home but he's a horse that needs somebody special to look after him. You'll do that, won't you?"

"King will be mine?" said Matt in an awed voice. When Sam nodded solemnly, he grinned joyfully and said, "Can I start tomorrow?"

"Not till I'm on the train to Edmonton. But after that, don't forget that King will be counting on you."

"As if I ever would," said Matt.

He ran off to look for more tepee rings but Josie stood still. A hawk was soaring in lazy circles above her.

"That bird is a better flier than Jerry Muldoon or even Katherine Stinson," she said to Sam.

He was watching the hawk, too. "I especially like the way they tilt their wings just a little and catch the next bit of wind. They do it so perfectly."

"And they don't have to argue with anyone about where they fly, or when. They just do it," said Josie. "But we have to argue and explain and get permission to do things."

"You won't have to do that if you stick to what everyone else expects you to do," said Sam.

"I'll have to argue," said Josie. "Jerry Muldoon says I'm cut out of the same cloth as Katherine Stinson. I think that means I'll get an idea in my head and go after it, no matter what." She stretched her arms high over her head and then as far wide as she could reach. "I just don't quite have the idea yet. But I will. Yes, I will."

Also by
CELIA BARKER LOTTRIDGE

Ticket to Curlew

WINNER
* Canadian Library Association
Book of the Year Award
* Geoffrey Bilson Historical Fiction Award

It is 1915, and Sam Ferrier and his father arrive by train in Curlew, Alberta, to build a new home for the family. When they finally reach their parcel of land, Sam can see nothing but endless stretches of grassland and blue sky. It is nothing like their old home in Iowa, and he wonders why his restless father ever decided to bring the family to this lonely, barren land.

In time, though, the house is built, and the rest of the family joins them. Gradually Sam discovers that there is much more to the flat and featureless prairie than he realized. The tall grasses hide a mysterious collection of gleaming white skulls. Torrential thunderstorms appear with startling swiftness out of a clear-blue sky. And when one day he finds that his little brother has suddenly disappeared on the seemingly flat prairie, Sam discovers that their new land can be both awesome, and frightening.

ISBN 0-88899-163-0 (hardcover)
ISBN 0-88899-221-1 (paperback)